LOGUE JAM

Paul Kindlon

Logue Jam
By Paul Kindlon

Hekate Publishing First Edition, 2020
ISBN: 978-1-912017-49-2
Hekate Publishing
73 John Drive
Farmingville, NY 11738
anthony_knott@hekatepublishing.com
https://www.hekatepublishing.com

The following acknowledgements list the work with original source in italics:

Rhetorical Question – *Random Sample*
Monster in the Lake – *The Opiate magazine*
Aphorisms and Eggshells – *TL; DR*
Secrets, Mysteries and Magic: A Personal Journey through Speculative Freemasonry and Beyond – *Former People*
Ars Poetica; Poor Players – *The Pangolin Review*
It's the Law; Cosmic Evolution – *Grey Sparrow*
The Ideal Woman; Stupid Mouse – *Big Windows Review*
Soul Music - *Harbinger Asylum*
"It's all relative of course" – *Fish Food Magazine*

These remaining works were all published in *Mystery Tribune:*
The Usurper
Agenbite of Inwit
Autumn Leaves
Bad Timing
Death imitates Art
Etiology of a Tragedy
Late Night Robbery
Matryoshka
One Day
So Many Thieves
True Detective
We are not amused
Scene… of the Crime
Alpha Male
Pain Killers
Last Fox Trot in San Francisco
King of Ithaca

Table of Contents

INTRODUCTION

Logue Jam is Paul Kindlon's exquisite initiation ceremony, with secret handshakes, chance meetings of the kindred, both on and off stage, missed cues and retraced steps. He constructs and deconstructs. The author is fascinated by how we think, by the thinkers themselves and closed societies. He introduces us to inbred royals and invites us to travel to the locations of their banishment. His players and quips are odd and captivating, his landscape tilted, not unlike the fictional town of Twin Peaks, where the comic delivers one liners to a half filled locals bar, nobody paying attention, the band's drummer answering with snare roll and tap on the ride. Kindlon, having worked in Chicago theater, earned a Phd in philosophy, served as journalist then professor at an American university in Moscow, has journeyed to Siberia, into the Arctic and back, embraces the un-conventional. He presents aphorisms, plays, short stories and poems, his force that through the green fuse drives the flower. He has seen many winters transform into spring and come full circle:

"As I prepare to turn another corner, I am hopeful still. I pray the right angle will lead me to something quite new. But if it doesn't, that's okay too. I realize this all must continue."

In the fifties, American writers were not allowed to be members of the Communist Party. They could, but at peril to their career. Today writers are again censored or rather, undergo more of an electronic filtering. To break certain rules of conduct, etiquette even, to present assemblages for publication may disallow them entry into what is uncertain. There are standard pathways with acceptable and unacceptable ways to rebel. There are too many of them for one, giving rise to a sub society with its own credentialing and reward systems, short of issuing magnetic thrall collars or implanting chips, digitized time stamping: The writer thrusts forward their wrist at the border, confirming tuition has been paid and that other preferences are in alignment and with a nod, the gate is lifted and they are allowed to pass into the party. Real inhomogeneity, what doesn't fit or ill understood, is snubbed, deemed unpublishable by many presses. In that regard, my favorite portion of Paul's compendium is *Secrets, Mysteries and Magic: A Personal Journey through Speculative Freemasonry and Beyond (A Memoir which is 99% true…)* also appealing as its organized in episode format.

The author might as well be writing by candlelight, his context appearing not so much of this time as another: Part drawing room thespian, muscovite, and De Quincey's Confessions of an English Opium Eater kind of guy. He has rambled, circumnavigated, sauntered and observed the motions of time.

Recalling Stein's description of Jim:

"He is romantic - romantic," he repeated. "And that is very bad - very bad ... very good, too," he added "But is he?" I queried. "Gewiss," he said, and stood still holding up the candelalbrum, but without looking at me. "Evident! What is it that by inward pain makes him know himself? What is it that for you and me makes him - exist?" (Lord Jim Chapter 20)

Paul Kindlon jumped. This unusual man did something unexpected, and here we have his new beginning.

Rhetorical Question

Who was that who ran wildly after school instead of playing
war with Timmy and opened the bird cage so Willy could fly
about freely, but especially so he could follow you around
fluttering happily above and behind his favorite kid in the
whole house while you led him down the corridor and through
the hallway to your bedroom whose door was open until you
slammed it shut knowing full well that Willy was right behind
ready to enter with you, but who came crashing into the
suddenly
closed door instead bashing his tiny blue head with a bump
you could hear as you stopped inside the room where no one
but you knew what happened or why and where you stood
in awe and shock as if surprised by the effect you intended
but now regret because you're not that way or so you thought
until this moment as you fear the consequences after mom
finds out which will be soon so you hide and pretend you
don't know while you wait for the bird to be found hopefully
alive because you don't want it to die really or so you try to
convince yourself as footsteps draw near and a frightening
scream is heard which forces you to open the door and see the
work you've done on the floor with its feathered torso
breathing heavily as if trying to pump back more life by
filling up with more air while you watch with remorse and a
sickening feeling that maybe you do know who you are as
mom takes the bird into her palms and carries him back to his
cage telling you that you should have been more careful
because birds have wings and need unhindered space to fly
through freely, you see, which is something you knew
all along, but you act like this is fresh news and express
your regret hoping that maybe Willy will make it through
with only a few bruises, but when you see him lying in his
cage with weakened eyes and breathing slower now you
know that soon your soul will change forever and that you'll
have to live with the fact that you murdered an innocent
animal who loved you – even sang for you – and who still,
even at this late stage, stares at you in wonder with a

puzzled look on his broken face and beads of blood slowly
dripping down over sad sleepy eyes that finally close
making you burst into tears as your mother consoles you
without having the slightest idea that she gave birth six
years ago to a monster who still has the power to close
a door quickly at any time.

Pep Talk to the Night Crew

"Pride, people! That's what it's all about. Pure unadulterated pride.
You know the feeling. When you finish your shift in the early morning and glance back at the work you've done. Floors all shiny and clean. Polished and buffed so well you could swear you're in a King's palace. Well, it just takes your breath away, doesn't it ?
My brothers and sisters...why are you here?
You are here because you're special... and unique.
Dedicated to the pursuit of excellence. Unwilling to leave behind a single speck of dust - or dare I say it - a smudge of dirt.
You have the talent and ability to transform a scuffed and stained
floor into a smooth and gleaming walkway.
You have the power to remove past mistakes in a process of glorious renewal...negating careless acts and uncultured habits with a masterful sweep of the broom. Creating order... where just minutes before absolute chaos reigned. Your loving hands methodically and carefully returning beauty to the floor and respect
for those who labored to produce these hallowed tiles.
And so I say to you "bravo". Bravo for being so demanding... so uncompromising. And so damn good!
Now...I'll let you in on a big secret...this company...this company NEEDS you. Our very strength is derived from you and your efforts. But especially from your superior attitude. You who are here - all of you - set the tone for our entire organization. That's right. Across the entire spectrum. Is it any wonder we share your values and beliefs?
Speaking of sharing...let me share a little story with you.
Just the other day, the Vice-President of our company said to me,
"Johnson. God darn it! I would trade in three of my top executives
for just one of your people."
And you know what I said? Do you know what I told him?

I said "Forget it J.G. These people are mine...Mine! "
I won't try to hide my affections. Why should I? You and I have been together a long time. We are bonded. I trust you explicitly and you better believe you can trust me because THAT is what it's all about, isn't it ?
But enough talk! Let's go out there and do it! Show them who's the best! Clean those babies until they sparkle and shine - like you - stars in the night!"
"Mr. Johnson…"
"Yes?"
"We're going on *strike*."

Ars Poetica

In this trying time of open-toed politics
late-night Mama jumpers
and flash-flood memories
I swear...
if I had a crown of thorns
I'd wear it sideways on a Sunday afternoon.

Secrets of Don Juan

Would you be surprised to learn that I was seduced as a child by nature? My one true love.
My first sensual experiences occurred during the summer – at night – when I would remove my
shoes and socks and slide my naked feet slowly through the grass of my front lawn.
In the morning mist I became fascinated by pretty little butterflies flirting with my eyes.
Their graceful movements hypnotized me. Forcing me to pursue and capture them.
To stroke their soft wings with the tip of a finger and then release. For one should not
covet beauty. That would be possessive and selfish. Let them be free to captivate others.
As time went by I became utterly enthralled by thunderstorms. Special – because they are
frightening, unpredictable and temporary. Like a mad woman filled with passion. Available to
all, but suddenly yours for just one night. Heavenly darkness with brief flashes of light. How you
love those black moments. When it seems like life itself is threatened. Proof of nature's power
and rule. And you the native son.
The sound of thunder like an orgasm you want to hear again and again. But louder.
Followed by a calm so disappointing you grow silent from the shock. At the rude awareness that
the thunder has stopped. And only short memories remain.
You start to move away...though you know the rainbow wants you to stay. But you feel
abandoned
By the swirling wind, by the fire in the sky, by the chance to defy death.
She doesn't understand.
Her skies are blue. No wonder it hurts.

Agenbite of Inwit

Jason waited until his grandfather was finished listening to the latest reports on the radio about the invasion of Normandy before approaching him.

"Grand pa I'm coming to you because I need your advice. I've decided to write something and well…who would know better than you.

"You wish to write?"

"Yes… I know I'm only thirty, but I want to begin writing my autobiography so my nieces, nephews and grandchildren can read about my life. I wrote one chapter, but realized I wasn't being totally forthcoming or honest. So instead of a conventional memoir I've decided to try something revolutionary. I'm going to write an autobiography as a sort of big crossword puzzle and the clues will all be about my life!"

"That's been done already"

"Really? By whom?"

"A fellow by the name of James Joyce"

"Imagine that. Is it any good?"

"It's considered to be the greatest novel written in the English language. It's also the most narcissistic, self-indulgent work ever produced by a guilt-ridden Irish Catholic mind.

Hemingway is just as bad. He writes autobiographical stories and then just changes the names of people. And as a reward for this subterfuge he is lionized. It's an insult! If one is going to be autobiographical at least be as good as Fitzgerald. And if you're writing a novel make it a novel by providing a plot. In a good novel the plot thickens; in Joyce's work 'Ulysses' it remains razor thin. Consider this nonsense: A Jewish man who has been cuckolded spends the day roaming around Dublin, entertains dirty thoughts about a club foot girl on the beach, goes to the

red light district and drinks, meets a young man and brings him home later where he entertains
the idea of having the young man engage in sex with his wife. The End"
"Do you know James Joyce?"
"Knew him. He was covertly murdered three years ago. But not a single soul knows about it"
"Grand pa you're not making sense. If no one knows about it then how could you possibly
know?…Grand pa?...Oh God, I'm sorry Gramps…I didn't mean to hurt your feelings."

Autumn Leaves

In the autumn, leaves not only fall to the ground – they become nature's toilet paper. All sorts of scatological substances adhere to their surfaces from bird and squirrel droppings to actual dog excrement. Examining them it is possible to detect remnants of tobacco from discarded cigarette butts, specks of dirt and strands of hair all contaminated by local pollutants.

Fearing this toxic mixture, Mr. Green carefully shuffled along during his morning and evening walks outside the Senior Citizens' home. The leaves – he was certain – were aware of his suspicious attitude towards them. Indeed…the leaves always sensed his presence and conspired to make his constitutional an unpleasant one. Following him menacingly. When he would turn around to confront a pair of leaves sneaking up on him they would suddenly veer away as if the wind had randomly changed direction.

He was much too old to be intimidated by anything or anyone. He proudly stood his ground and defiantly kicked away any offending leaf that tried to block his path.

The day after Halloween he took his usual stroll and discovered it was quite windy and wet.

Puddles had formed overnight. While turning the corner he slipped on an oak leaf and fell off the sidewalk. He knew he had hit the ground rather hard, but there was thankfully no sign of pain. While on his back an elm leaf climbed onto his forehead and two leaves entered deep into his mouth covering his wind pipe.

His right hand was pinned underneath his torso while his left hand struggled to to grasp his cane just out of reach. Complicating matters was the fact he had landed awkwardly

with his left foot – the good one – caught in a drainage ditch. He struggled to lift himself, but was
distracted by another leaf that landed on his right eye – the good one. Now almost blind, he tried
to call out for help and a gust of wind blew another leaf into his mouth. He was squirming on the
muddy ground and turned his head sideways hoping to dislodge a leaf or two only to see a worm
taunting him. Flying leaves gathered around his neck. Others began to cover his ears muffling
the outside world. Tired of the battle he eventually gave in and surrendered as another downpour
commenced.
The autopsy showed that he had died of natural causes.

Bad Timing

Sasha thought it was a good idea. Samson did too. Only Carol – the skeptic - wasn't sure.

Jesus…it's like taking candy from a baby. I've noticed that most of them don't even lock their doors because they want the EMS people to have quick and easy access if they should suffer a heart attack. Another thing is the old ladies generally keep their jewelry in a special drawer somewhere in their bedrooms. And many of these people have money stashed away in their apartments. I don't know if it's because they don't trust banks or their relatives, but a lot of them keep money in their freezers.

Something's wrong, Sasha…or I mean missing…it seems too easy. There has to be a weakness somewhere in you plan…something you're not taking into account.

Like what?

Oh I don't know. What if – when we enter their door- they have a heart attack right then and there. Are you gonna rob somebody who is having a heart attack that you are the cause of?

Wow, she's right Sasha. What about that? Makes sense to me.

Okay genius…if it's a bad idea then you tell me one that's better.

I will. "Honesty is the best policy".

After Samson explained his idea both Sasha and Carol agreed to go along.

Sasha's job was to guard the hallway near the elevator and be the look –out.

Samson tapped lightly on the first door and slowly opened it.

An elderly gentleman asked who he and Carol were.

We're robbers here to steal from you, but don't be afraid. We will not hurt you at all. I promise you.

The gentleman seemed surprised, but not shocked and nodded his head in quiet

resignation.
His wife appeared to find out who was visiting at such a late hour. When her husband
told her who these people were and why they were there, her reaction was that of
annoyance.
Where is your jewelry?
I'll get it for you, but you're not getting my wedding ring! She then proceeded to her
bedroom and re-appeared carrying jewelry - draped over a pistol. While Samson was
busy emptying the refrigerator of frozen Benjamins, Mrs. Mortimer shot Carol right
through the heart.
Samson – terrified and traumatized – fled the scene screaming.
The sleepy neighbors came out to see who was making such a ruckus.
Sometime later, a policeman questioned Mrs. Mortimer.
If I understand you correctly…you shot the intruder because they had the audacity to rob
you at night?
Not just any night. Today is Tuesday and they came here at nine-o'clock. That got me all
riled up. Everyone knows that's when my program is on!

Death Imitates Art

The creative idea was Henderson's, but his bosses agreed to the crazy idea – a re-enactment of "War of the Worlds" on a live broadcast with actors. Only this time the script would be more realistic. Instead of Martians, America would be invaded by Chinese and Russians.

How was Henderson to know it would all go so badly?

The concept itself made a ton of sense, really. A big marketing ploy to boost ratings and crush the competition.

Sitting at home with his old dog by his side on the floor, judge Wendell Principle flipped on the TV to watch his favorite reality show. It was interrupted only five seconds in by an urgent news bulletin that made the judge drop his remote. Right on top of Rusty.

The neighbors would have heard Wendell uncharacteristically screaming, but they were busy doing the same. It was that kind of night. Historical and life changing.

Most people believed the special report unquestioningly leading to chaos and hysteria.

Sitting at home in his mansion with his Persian cat on his lap, was Mallory Gibbons III laughing like a maniac at the news report. After all, it was Gibbons who hired Henderson to write the script and then convince the execs at the rival network to go along.

A brilliant plan executed to perfection.

The acting was very believable, but if the audience had only waited for the break following ten minutes of fictitious news, they would have learned that it was all a staged drama. Thousands left their home immediately, however, and proceeded to rape, steal and murder.

There was absolute mayhem on a warm summer night.

The network that aired the hoax would be out of business in less than a month. Naturally.

Henderson disappeared into the ether. And Mallory Gibbons' role was never uncovered. In fact, his cable TV shows saw their ratings jump as noted journalists and intelligence experts took sides debating whether Henderson had fled to Russia or China. In reality, Henderson was hiding in neither place. Five years after the broadcast he was found dead on a remote island in the Hebrides after eating some haggis that was contaminated by a lethal pathogen.

Utterly fatal.

Just Maria

After the tragedy, friends expressed shock and disbelief. What the authorities were saying
couldn't possibly be true. It just couldn't. Maria was not that way. But apparently she was.
The community reacted with both revulsion and heart ache mixed with a morbid curiosity.
How could such a thing happen to this ideal couple from two very prominent families?
The tragedy makes one question basic fundamental assumptions concerning the sacred bonds that are formed between loved ones.
Maria grew up on a grand estate where she was free to ride horses and tend a small garden. Her
father even bought her a flock of fine Shetland sheep – four precious lambs.
At twenty-one came courtship leading to marriage. Her beautiful beau had many young ladies
trying to capture his heart, but he only wanted Maria. Just her.
After the wedding Maria had delayed having a child for twelve years because she wanted to
maintain her splendid figure. Then came Conchita…followed by the dreaded pouch that just
would not go away.
After fifteen years of marriage, her husband left her for a young exotic beauty. Maria – quite
frankly – lost it. She couldn't deal with it. But she did…in a bad way.
Her tall and handsome husband had not only abandoned her, but humiliated her. Deeply.
So she planned revenge. And then carried it out. At Conchita's birthday party.
She had arranged to purchase a special white piñata fashioned after her daughter's favorite Disney character - Dumbo.
When the little girl whacked away at the piñata blindfolded a terrible explosion occurred. The father – they say – would remain inconsolable for the rest of his life, poor soul.
Maria immediately fled the scene of the disaster and went straight to the airport ticket in hand.

After a refreshing Pina Colada at the bar, she boarded a flight for Athens where, upon arrival,
she discovered that she was apparently wanted.

Etiology of a Tragedy

Her alarm was set as usual at 7 AM, but Nora awoke earlier that October morning when Fluffy –
a birthday present from her granddaughter - made whimpering noises by her bedside. Although it
was only six o'clock, some pre-dawn light was already peeking through the kitchen window
providing a modest contrast with the still darkened bedroom down the hallway where she put on
her blue robe and pink slippers.
After visiting the bathroom to relieve herself, she promised Fluffy a quick walk in the park
before breakfast so that her "little stinker" might do the same. Nora clicked on the coffeemaker
that had been filled up the night before and got dressed to go outside.
Anticipating the visit to the park, Fluffy began to bark and Nora had to shush her a few times
so as not to awaken the neighbors. The Finleys were late risers and "not the friendliest people in
the world". Unlike Benson the door man who always had a smile.
Fluffy went about her business almost immediately and returned to her owner with a big smile or
so it seemed to Nora. About half-way through the park they strolled as birds sang and squirrels
jumped from tree to tree like professional acrobats in the big top.
Nora's sense of wonder and well-being was disturbed, however, by a figure in the distance that
she could not quite make out. It wasn't the paperboy – *that* she knew.
Her old fears began to resurface and her hands shook as she held Fluffy's leash tighter.
It was a black man – she was sure – and he was heading straight for her. Running at full speed
half-naked. Oh God…the trauma resurfaced. A childhood episode she thought she thought she
had overcome years ago. But no… all the fear and terror of that day returned in a torrent

of vivid memories. The screams, the panic, the pain, the feeling of being abandoned by God and the world all at once. As the black man raced towards her he seemed to be in a state of extreme excitation for he was breathing heavily, arms flailing. A wild man. Fluffy began barking loudly, but she was only a tiny Maltese. Hardly a source of protection.

Nora felt a sharp pain – was it a knife that he held to her throat now piercing her neck? And then it felt as though her rib cage was being squeezed by two powerful vice-like arms.

As she lost consciousness she could see the black man stop just a few feet away with a look of fearful astonishment. He bent down to check Nora's pulse as Fluffy continued barking. The early morning sunlight filtered through the red and yellow leaves and softly illuminated Nora's face as the nervous jogger made an emergency call on his phone.

The following weeks would be filled with conversations by Nora's relatives searching for the clues to the cause of this tragedy. But even we who have full knowledge of the incident cannot be sure of the main cause. Was it not an instance of unlucky chance? Or was it simply old age and a weakened heart? Was it due, perhaps, to the trauma she suffered earlier on in life? Or should we pin the blame on Fluffy? It was the little stinker, after all, who had to go pee early making it possible for the chance encounter with Leon who had been hired by the granddaughter.

Late Night Robbery

My life has been one disappointment after another.
I grew up alone with my single hippie Mom Abby. When I reached an age where I finally
got up the courage to ask who my father was, she replied.
"I don't know…. Napoleon!" and then laughed like Shirley MacClaine.
On my sixteenth birthday she gave me hot cocoa and ice cream cake followed by a present.
I unwrapped the box and looked inside.
"Mom! Extra large condoms?
"Don't worry...you'll grow into them,"she said
When I finally got my B.A. in Greek Mythology after six years of serious struggle, I knew I was
pretty much screwed. And my student loan debt was like a sword of Damocles swinging
like a pendulum over my head.
Tough times call for tough guys.
I never saw myself as a criminal, but I was about to do something decidedly unlawful.
Knowing there was a well-to do neighbor down the street, I decided I would rob him and his
exotic Roma wife of both money and jewelry. At gunpoint. A cliché I know, but I was desperate.
Rule number one of robbery is "don't get caught".
Rule number two is "use lethal force if necessary"
I always follow the rules, but I was hoping to skip number two.
To make sure I would not be recognized I hatched a clever plan.
On the day of the robbery after I bought a gun and bullets, I went to "Lola's Costume Shop" and
purchased a Halloween mask of Vladimir Putin. Very menacing I thought. As I approached the
home of my victims I kept practicing lines appropriate to the circumstance at hand.
At exactly 10:30 P.M. Mister moneybags himself opened the door.
I pushed him inside and looked around for any unwelcome guests.
"What do you want?!" he said on cue.

It was then that I pulled out the handgun and uttered my lines with a terrifying Russian accent.
"Geeve me your money or I vill keel you and your Gypsy vife!"
My victim immediately bent down, touching his knees, and began laughing hysterically.
This was not going according to script.
He then grabbed a note pad, sat down, and began furiously scratching away.
"This is crazy!" he screamed in delight.
You're telling me.
He explained that he was a comedy writer and was late with a deadline. "I'm going to use this!
he told me. "I was at my wit's end…couldn't come up with a good idea. You saved my life!
If I hadn't produced a new skit by midnight Lorne would've killed me!"

Pain Killers

Simon and Peter made a pact. Having worked in the field of medical science for over a decade and seeing the tragedy unfold in the country with pain killer addiction they decided to take action to counteract the epidemic, albeit on a small scale.

Knowing they could not take on the entire social tragedy they chose to focus on a related matter: morphine usage among the terminally ill.

Both gentlemen were of the opinion that it was equally tragic to have patients suffering from a prolonged illness routinely administered this powerful opiate which relieved pain, but left one with a false reality - an unusual sense of well-being, a relaxed and calm feeling that is essentially a lie. Simon and Peter felt that this practice was actually de-humanizing although everyone claimed it was the most humane way to treat suffering patients.

Treating terminally ill patients in this manner robbed them of their dignity, turning each patient into a junkie incapable of thinking or feeling clearly. It was one step removed from a vegetative state. Human beings deserve better, they believed. So they worked on a way to provide a welcome release from the physical and psychological pain.

Simon and Peter perfected a method using an organic mixture that shuts down the body's vital organs in minutes, but that no pathologist in the world would be able to detect as the cause of death. For their clients, this was of utmost importance because none wanted to be remembered as having committed suicide – assisted or not.

Customers came to them only by word of mouth. Most were cancer patients ready to take the plunge. What these clients all had in common was that they did not want their families to suffer anymore and that the news of their death would be reported as natural. Simon and Peter could guarantee that and the cost was not prohibitive.

Despite precautions and the very covert nature of their operations, they were eventually caught and put on trial. The news media portrayed the pair as modern day Kevorkians and their detractors called them "Doctors of Death". Supporters, however, likened them to romantic idealists carrying out a Quixotic campaign.

Their story went national and then international. Perhaps because of this, Simon and Peter were able to obtain a top-notch defense team working pro-bono. All three were Harvard grads.

There was no relevant evidence presented, but the testimony of key witnesses was overwhelming and quite damning. And then this happened. Quite unexpectedly…

The proceedings were abbreviated and a "mistrial" was declared. According to law, this meant that the pair would not have to face a re-trial owing to the constitutional clause of "double jeopardy". Simon and Peter were free men.

In an ironic twist of fate, the presiding judge passed away just two months later following a long illness.

Matryoshka

I am an editor and I've decided to write a story about a writer writing a story about an editor who
wrote a story about a writer.
But that's not important. The important thing is to finish this damn assignment that just landed
on my desk.
My boss wants me to cover a story about an eighty year-old man who has been living in a tree
for fifty years. That means I'll have to interview this local Tarzan. I do hope he bathes.
Before I go, however, I bang out two pages of my own story. Double spaced. In it, the editor has
just hired a beautiful secretary. And they fall in love. The only problem is . . . the secretary is
married. To a writer. A very jealous writer it turns out because the jealous husband will attack
his wife's lover and cut off one of his ears.
I leave my office and go downstairs to pick up a pack of cigarettes and who do I see buying Juicy
Fruit? The secretary who's married to the jealous husband. She looks like Veronica Lake.
"Good Moring handsome", she says to me.
"Oh..you. Didn't notice you."
"Well I noticed you. In fact, I think I may like you… newspaper boy. Like you a lot."
She hands me a stick of gum and says, "chew on that"
I checked out her ass as she walked away. It was time well spent.
"So sassy!" I say to myself.
"POISON"
I turned around to the cashier and asked, "Did you just call her poison?"
"Oh no, man. I said 'poisson'. I'm studying French. It means fish."
Well that settled it. I decided to go to "Flipper's" for a fish fry and then to the jungle to visit
Tarzan.
Jesus! What a day. Tarzan refused to talk to me. But I found a gentleman who claims he's been
friends with Tarzan for forty years. So, I interview him instead.

"Okay…so who is this guy living up in the tree?"
"He came from Great Britain originally. Studied at Harvard and decided to settle here. Never married though."
"So what happened to him?"
"Well, it seems as though he had a perfect life. Then one day he made fun of the Super Bowl and lost all his friends. Lost his job, too"
"Because of the Super Bowl?"
"I think so. He worked in Advertising. Said he was an editor. The loss of job and friends really threw him for a loop. He began to fall apart…completely lost it."
"How so?"
"Apparently, he decided to write a story about a writer writing a story about an editor who wrote a story about a writer."
The friend reached into his pocket.
"Here. This is a copy of the story he wrote"
I took a look. It was two pages long. Double spaced.

It’s the Law

Justice is blind
It's the golden rule
but if you're rich
she'll manage a peak
and give you a wink
Mad about that girl!

One Day

Little Mary grew up poor. The kind of poor that just breaks your heart. Years of living in a trailer
home with an Irish dad and Cherokee mom – both of them heavy drinkers. Double whammy. Her
daddy died one day. Shot himself. Little Mary heard it all cause she was in the next room when it
happened. The sound was so loud it shook the whole trailer.
Life got harder for her mom after that. She had no money and no job. Then one day her momma
brought home an Uncle Joe. . That was a relative she had never heard of before. This Uncle Joe
would occasionally stay over. He was not awfully friendly, but he was very kind. Her momma
got gifts and flowers and there was a lot more food in the fridge.
One day in spring, at breakfast, Momma told little Mary that Uncle Joe had a wonderful present
for her this time round. All she had to do was to meet him at the Post Office in town and he'd
give her a brand new fur coat! Mary didn't even finish her grits and honey – her favorite. She
practically flew out the door cause she couldn't wait. When she came back home about an hour
later, little Mary was very upset and close to tears. As she walked through the door her momma
cried out "April Fools!"
Now… twenty years later to the very day someone killed little Mary's mom. I was with her the
night it happened. We were eating at a fancy restaurant and did a few shots together. We both got
a bit tipsy. Mary started to tell me about her new home.
"Did you know in Japan", she said to me, "if someone tells you that you're the smartest person in
the world it's actually not a compliment."
When the waiter asked about dessert Mary said…" You have hot apple pie?"
"Yes, Maam," he replied.
"Good, I'll have that, but serve it to me cold".
Later…when the waiter brought the check she turned to him and said, "do you want a tip?"

The waiter kind of laughed and said, "Well, yes Ma'am I sure wouldn't mind."
Mary then says, "Don't bet on the horses!"
That poor boy walked away with his tail 'tween his legs.
When the bill came it was almost a hundred dollars.
Mary put down four hundred dollars on the table and left a note that said, "Buy yourself a new coat."

Poor Players

The bard perceived the entire world as a stage because we all do.
Drawn by the colored lights, no doubt,
we linger long and only the few seek a quick exit.
Itinerant puppets wearied of the playwright's string,
they hope never again to have to wait in the wings.

Soul Music

If I could be born again, I'd want to be black. Don't you?
And if I were a woman I'd only hang out with black dudes.
I'd have them sing Motown tunes
night and day.
The ones that make romance sound so sexy... so irresistible...
Mmmm... that sweet stuff !
Yet here I am enslaved in this silly – white - skin. Pale imitation
of the real thing. Truth is I'm jealous. Can't play it off .
They have what I don't. And now I got it bad.
I want to dance without fear. Move my hips in a sensuous way.
Drive the ladies wild. I want to laugh loudly. Kiss with big lips
Feel the jazz in my finger tips.
I got the Blues all ready !

I order my heart to pound a tribal beat. Primitive and
uncivilized.
I demand the right to be a natural born man.
To kill that clown who stands white in my place.
I raise a black fist - clenched in defiance.
I'm Malcolm!
Stokely!
Maybe even Nat Turner!
Put chains on my feet. Whip me till I bleed.
Give me a reason to scream - cry out - and rebel.
Make me black. Where I belong.
These are my people. Let me go !

I'm standing here in my darkness, but you just can't see.
Go ahead ... ignore me.
Better yet - hate me for the things I've said.
Make me feel unwanted and despised.
When you do...
I'll know you're Motown too.

So Many Thieves

Spencer-Kingsley: My dear Shaw. This experiment of mine will show that given the proper use of reward and punishment I can and will be able to transform my servant Molly from a virtuous Christian girl into a thief through what is called behavior modification. In short, I will have her steal an ancient Greek statue of a goddess that my neighbor Stanley has in his home.
George: If you succeed – and I doubt you will – how long will it take to transform your young servant?
Spencer-Kingsley: I can accomplish my goal I would say in less than three months.
George: If you are so confident my dear fellow, why not engage in a gentleman's wager?
Spencer-Kingsley: Indeed, why not?
After three months both gentlemen met again to discuss the outcome of the experiment.
The professor told of his initial frustration with the slow process of modifying the young servant's behavior, but discovered through patience and persistence, that he was finally able to get the young lady to steal the statue.
The professor used a series of rewards – mostly gifts and money to her and her family. He offered special medical treatment for her ailing father and the use of a carriage to and from work. To get Molly to break into a private home and abscond with a precious work of art, Spencer-Kingsley had to promise a new farmhouse for her and her family.
"And guess where she wants me to build it? On your bloody green island! But it's worth it. I'm contributing to the advancement of science. I've proven my point and won our bet. Oh here…"
The professor walked George over to a desk and opened a drawer. Inside was a beautiful statue of a Greek goddess.
George: Eee gads!
Spencer-Kingsley: Don't panic old boy. I intend on returning it tomorrow before Stanley and I play cricket.
George: Tell me…now that you know for sure that you have a thief in your midst will you let her go?
Spencer-Kingsley: Utterly impossible.
George: And why is that?

Spencer-Kingsley: Well you see…the thing is…I've fallen in love with her.

George: My word! That's certainly an unintended consequence of a scientific experiment.

Spencer-Kingsley: Yes, and it seems as though the experiment has transformed me as well.

George: Does that mean you no longer smoke cigars?

Spencer-Kingsley: It surely does not…shall we?

Both gentlemen retrieve a cigar from a specially designed box and light up.

Spencer-Kingsley: I say George…the success of this experiment has me wondering. Do you think I could take an uneducated ruffian off the streets of London and transform him into a proper English gentleman?

George: I think I may have an even better idea.

True Detective

Ed had been working as a detective now for five years. Joe was a twenty-five-year veteran.

Both were dedicated professionals. Curious and talkative.

"Say Ed…whatever made you choose this line of work anyhow?"

"Reading Sherlock Holmes. I was fascinated by his use of logic. Deduction to be precise.

You?"

"Perry Mason"

"He wasn't a detective; he was a lawyer. In fact, his name is an inside joke."

This was not fiction, however, but stark reality.

Today they had a warrant and a job to do. An investigation of a horrendous murder.

They were here to find out how… and maybe why. The who they already knew.

Her name was Jennifer Jones. Aged twenty-one. Single. A student. Yesterday was her very sad
funeral.

"Sixty nine Elmwood Avenue. Okay, this is it. I'm telling you Ed…when you can handle this…
this dark side of the human soul without breaking down, you know you've chosen the right
profession."

When Ed and Joe entered the bedroom they saw newspaper clippings on the wall of Ted Bundy's
heinous crimes. Apparently he was a fan. There was even a poster of the infamous
killer hanging above his bed.

"Who the hell sells posters of Ted Bundy?"

"Your Grandma…I don't know. There's a weirdo born every minute. What's this stuff?"

They discovered some special equipment in the far corner.

"The son of a bitch made the posters himself!"

"He made his own posters? Pretty clever guy."

As they investigated further they found a videotape with a note attached. It was addressed to
Joe and Ed.

"What the hell?"

"A personal note. Nice! Check the other side."
Sure enough. Written there were the following words…
"Hey guys. Had a great time! Hope you gentlemen enjoy this."
Ed put on the tape and pressed PLAY.
What the detectives saw was the actual murder. From start to finish. And beyond.
As the recording begins Ms. Jones can be seen sitting next to the guy. They kiss. And fondle.
And kiss again. Soon they are both naked and alive. But not for long.
He suddenly pulls her up and knocks her out cold with one massive blow. His figure then leaves
the frame only to return in a moment with a knife, slashing away. Blood begins to issue forth from multiple wounds as her slender body is bathed in red.
He is next seen putting on a CD.
As Ms. Jones continues bleeding, he picks her up off the carpet and waltzes with her around the
room.
"Damn, he's a good dancer", Joe remarks.
"I'm sure he has many fine qualities. Jesus Joe…he must really hate women."
"Not as much as he hates himself. What's that music? I can't make it out."
"Lady in Red. Chris de Burgh."
"Wow. I thought I had a sick sense of humor. This guy's on a whole nother level."

CLICK

"Ed?..."
"What?"
"Wanna see it again? "
"Sure."

We are not amused

Johnny just finished telling a joke about a cartoon character who was thrown from the top of a castle by an evil princess, but survived. *How* do you ask? Well, the punch line was "fate". No one laughed, except a young lady the bartenders call "Jan - without ice".

Janice so wanted to dance with Johnny - or "my little sweetie pie"- as she began calling him. But Johnny was reluctant, maybe even scared, and for good reason. So Janice had to "sweetie pie" him to death before he finally got up on the dance floor.

What a couple. Johnny was about half her size when she was in high heels and he seemed off balance most of the time, holding her down stretched hands and looking around as if in a trance. Perhaps he was. Still dreaming about this sudden new life with a normal girl who loves *him* and doesn't care that he's ...."a leprechaun".

A few days before, Johnny was a social non-entity. People ignored his presence like one does when standing next to some sad loser. Suddenly, however, God was no longer mean or cruel. Johnny, believe it or not, was finally at peace with himself and that other world.

Feeling confident after that first dance, the mixed couple dared to take center stage while the crowd drew back and watched Janice slide up and down Johnny's proud body in a rhythmic tease. Three songs in a row. He "had it too"; he was trying to tell them.

Enter fate without a partner. For as the applause subsided a hand reached out and violently grabbed Janice by the arm, right above Johnny's head. He turned to look up and noticed the furious face of Philip - or Janice's ex- as most people began to call him.

"Okay, Jan" Philip announced decisively. That's about enough. You proved your point. Let's go now"

Responding instinctively to the threat, Johnny jumped up like a crazed rabbit and produced "fisticuffs" in dire seriousness. The effect of seeing this determined David intent on bringing down Janice's Goliath was unfortunate, but real. From Johnny's perspective, the crowd's laughter seemed distant and muffled. Filtered through an old defense.

He staggered a bit and then - tragically - tripped over Janice's foot. Even *she* laughed as Johnny tumbled over like a circus clown.

Seizing the moment, Philip proceeded to give Johnny a hand - to help him up off the dance floor. As he did so, he grabbed one of Johnny's tempting little feet and began swinging him around through the air. The band - seeing *their* opportunity - began playing the tune to "Superman".

The crowd, of course, couldn't help themselves by now. It was simply too late.

Feeling responsible, Janice screamed for Philip to stop and he mercifully did. But rather abruptly. Johnny's head hit bottom and bounced. His eyeballs rattled in their sockets.

"Alright" she stated emphatically. "I'll go with you, if you leave him alone and Philip… don't ever dare touch this man again. Do you hear?"

"Fine with me"

From Johnny's perspective the crowd grew, but silently. He waved to them and the little leprechaun finally disappeared. His existence was no longer needed. Or funny.

Scene . . . of the Crime

" God damn. Lookey here. Whoooo…wee! Well I'll be….takes all kinds I guess."

"Shut up and tell me."

"I was a gonna. Keep your pants on there quick draw…the story - I mean- the story is just crazy.

That's just what it is. This fella who wrote this… says there was this thing called 'French naturlism' one time and that one time in a thee-ater in Paris an actor actually killed another actor live on stage. Seems like he used a loaded gun instead of a fake one in order to make the actin more realistic-like. Did the job that's for sure. Now I know actors can be strange…just look at Johnny Depp and that woman with the big lips…what's her name?"

"No idea."

"Don't matter. The fact is this here actor took things too far. To say the least. Kinda reminds me of you in a way, Catfish. Not to be critical, but you can sometimes cross the line buddy. I mean I love ya and all, but you need to tone it down a bit. You're too high-strung. And that ain't good.

Hell Catfish, just because I beat you at checkers don't mean you have to tip over the board for Christ's sake. It's only a dumb game after all. I can't help it if I'm lucky. I mean what happened at the track yesterday kinda proves it, don't it? You been following the horses for – what – ten years or so, right?

" Fifteen"

"So that's what I'm sayin. You bein a track veteran and me well…I had no idea what I was doin, but I won anyway. Same way with the ladies. It ain't my fault Betty Sue's been sweet on me.

Hell I know how you feel about her. But it's her choice. She just don't want you to court and spark her.

Sometimes things just don't work out buddy and you gotta deal with it. You ain't no fool you

dummy… you know what I'm talkin about. You can only play with the cards you been dealt.
The tables turn eventually, right?
I mean…I seem to have a good hand lately – that's true – Heck, I seem to draw Aces all the
time! That's bound to change though. It's a question of time, buddy. You'll see."
"Betty Sue let you kiss her?"
"Yessum. She sure did"
"Big kiss or little kiss?"
"I don't know. In-between maybe. A normal kiss. Now wait a second here. Why we talking
about this?"
"I just wanted to know…that's all. She let you do more than kiss her?"
"Whoa! Slow down there…that's kind of private-like don't ya think?"
" Then why'd you start talkin about it? Seems like you're bragging to me."
" Hell no… I ain't braggin...I was just tryin to explain things. That's all."
" You sure got a funny way of doin it."
" Why you shakin like that? You feel all right? "
"She's my girl!"
"Now hold on there…don't you think that maybe she should decide who she likes?"
"Oh she's gonna like me all right. I'll make sure of that."
"And how you gonna do that?"
"I got my ways…"
"Lord Jesus…Catfish…hey now…put that gun down. Catfish…no…wait…
Catfish! Don't do it!"

"The End"

Monster in the Lake

When my father began rowing the boat, I felt a surge of excitement.

"Dad! How long will it take to get there?"

"Maybe an hour."

"Oh. This water looks really deep."

"It is. I believe it goes down to around 500 feet in some places."

"Wow! Are there any monsters in the lake?"

"Ernest, that's just in fiction. Monsters only live in the imagination."

"Do you write about monsters?"

"Try not to. Actually, the island we're going to is where I wrote my best story. Unfortunately, it was never published."

"How come?"

"That's a very good question, son. I've often wondered about that. It had everything. Great style and structure. Believable characters. It was a story about an Indian woman who was pregnant and having trouble. A doctor came to help her give birth. After he assisted in the process, he discovered that the father had committed suicide just minutes before. Killed himself with a knife. You see death is a natural thing. Just like life. But it's also mysterious... almost as mysterious as the publishing game. You just never know."

"Dad...is dying hard? "

"To be honest, a lot of factors come into play. What a person's done, for example. Adventures. Scandals. Crazy lifestyle. A person can struggle for years without being noticed. Actually, writing is the easy part. Getting published is difficult."

"But Dad...what about dying?"

"Oh that...well of course it doesn't hurt. "

Love of Wisdom

Professor Stevenson taught Philosophy for twenty years at Harvard. Although he was pleased to impart knowledge and engage in conceptual argumentation with bright students, his real passion was the quest for wisdom. In particular, the professor wanted to know the ultimate truth which is, of course, *the meaning of life.*

This yearning for the secret of existence was increased ten-fold when he spent an afternoon with an Anthropology professor. His colleague told him of an enlightened sage living in the Himalaya Mountains. And moreover, it was possible to obtain an audience with him.

"But it will cost you. The gentlemen who do the arranging ask for nearly half a million dollars.

The money – I'm told – is used for humanitarian purposes the bulk of which goes to the United Nations."

"It's a small price to pay for wisdom", Stevenson replied.

An appropriate time was chosen for the trek to Tibet and a dangerous climb up the mountain.

Stevenson had a Sherpa who carried sleeping bags and sleeping pads, as well as food, a stove and two bottles of oxygen.

The professor carried water bottles, tea flasks, sunscreen, headlamp extra layers, camera, notepad, and gloves.

It took three days, but the pair reached their destination without incident. Stevenson was, however, feeling the effects of the high altitude. His Sherpa gave him oxygen and encouragement…

"You are on the right path, doctor. Come with me."

They entered a cavern that was fairly expansive. At the far end was a fire that blazed like a metaphor. Sitting behind the flames was indeed an old man with a beard and silver pentagram hanging from a sparkling chain.

"Welcome! It is good to see a fellow searcher."

"Thank you."
"Do you have a question, professor?"
"Yes…yes I do. I have to know…I need to know… the meaning of life."
"Oh that. Yes of course. There are many meanings, in fact. Each person has a meaning all their own. It is for *you* to decide what that meaning is!"
"That's it? I've traveled all this distance to hear some Buddhist existentialism? Should I clap with one hand now? This is outrageous!"
At that moment the Sherpa snuck up from behind and struck the professor on the head with a blunt instrument. One more victim to the treacherous slopes of the Himalayas.
"Let's get out of here." The Sherpa reached into his pocket and produced a wad of money.
"Your cut. Good job."
The old wise man raised a fist full of one hundred grand and shaking it at the professor bellowed,
"This is the meaning of life you dumbass!"
His booming voice was a bit too loud, though. It echoed and reverberated beyond the cavern and created an avalanche.
Alas…
It took a year to uncover the three frozen bodies. The search team – after vigorous debate – decided to split the money.

Aphorisms and Eggshells

Unrequited love: A heart that is paying dearly while Cupid is being frugal.

I once employed the work ethic, but it didn't work for me.

Mediocrity dances to the rhythm of routine.

Comme il faut: Not eating frogs' legs during leap year.

Landlord: One who comes up with astronomical figures by calculating with the space by time formula.

Most men lead lives of quiet desperation – unless they happen to be your neighbors.

I've had so many ups and downs the buttons on my coat have numbers on them.

Thanks to the very trendy plumber out-houses are now in.

Double meaning: when a pregnant pause gives birth to twins.

Stoicism: when – in the face of adversity – you can keep a stiff upper lip
And not even raise an eyebrow as you take it on the chin.

Only a Buddhist can find soul food in an empty refrigerator.

In true love there is no difference between giving and taking.
And then she leaves you.

Temptation is everywhere – so there's really no need to travel.

Every cloud has a silver lining, but the damn things leak anyway.

When you die people pay their last respects.
Unfortunately, you're in no condition to collect.

France – they say – is sublimely civilized.

So why is their national holiday a prison riot?

Terminal illness is the alarm clock of spiritual awakening.

Tell your wife your secrets and she will praise you for your honesty. All my wives have done so.

The size of the universe indicates a clear case of substance abuse.

Behind every great man is a woman…trying to hide from his wife.

Learn from your mistakes and in the future, you will be much less ignorant
when you repeat them.

Marriage: A whisper that begins and ends with a shout.

Live as though you have a hole in your shoe. It will make you more attentive to what others are thinking and saying and conscious of every step you take.

Platonic relationship: An imperfect copy of the Ideal.

When political opinion is formed by a majority coalition of fear and ignorance it can always defeat the undemocratic truth.

The doctoral dissertation is a challenge because, after having spent 25 years on the knees of ventriloquists, they then expect you to find your own voice.

It's absurd to think we should know beforehand what will happen to us after death. That would be like explaining a joke before the punch line is delivered.

Crisis management: intervening to untie knots for those who are at the end of their rope.

"The way to a man's heart is through his stomach": Advice of an older woman intended to mislead her younger competition.

Low self-esteem: Giving yourself a bad review before you even begin to act.

Misanthrope: One who sits in judgment while standing aloof.

Non-sequitur: The shortest distance between two points.

Practice makes perfect – especially in theory.

Moral dilemma: Deciding whether or not to cancel an appointment with sin because of the unexpected punctuality of conscience.

If you allow them to put a collar around your soul and hold it by a leash, you may as well let them bury your bones.

Over-confidence: Giving yourself credit at the expense of others.

Racism: One mutt accusing another mutt of having a pedigree.

A woman's orgasm is like a good joke. Once you've heard it you can't wait to repeat it.

Male narcissism: When a woman can charm the pants off you and make you lose your shirt because you're convinced that she adores you in your birthday suit.

People who do not exercise their wills are like seeing-eye dogs for the blind forces of nature.

Optimists believe that chaos is just temporarily out of order

If you can read the writing on the wall, you're probably developing bad spelling habits.

Originality is the loner we all fear.

First and foremost, an artist tries to paint what he sees in his mind. If that fails, he then goes out of his mind.

Charity takes the color out of your cheeks.

Psychologists say that intellectual ideas alone cannot cause mental problems.
Such pronouncements, of course, are symptomatic of genius envy.

Deception is a woman's defense against the perceived threat of having to acknowledge that she's just as foolish as a man.

Philosophy is the work of great magicians being tricked by their own illusions.

Hedonism is often spiritual foreplay.

What we call wisdom is usually just infectious self-deception.

Experience may be a great teacher, but an education can be quite costly.

Fond remembrance is an attempt to assure ourselves the present is valuable and the future worth enduring.

Arrogance shows when a strip tease of the Ego bares all.

When extended, the bridge between childhood and adulthood can take a heavy toll.

I was destined for greatness, but when my fate got distracted my luck ran out.

Boredom is a jealous ghost hovering over your soft little soul with devil dust and bad intentions.

If you build a better mousetrap some little rat will be sure to file suit.

Bartender's nightmare: A sudden ambush by revenge-minded water spirits lurking in the shadowy stains of carelessly spilled ancestors.

I remember as a child when religion was a pillow for my soul filled with the feathers of angels.

Patience without anticipation quickly becomes neglect.

Talent can be poisonous ... if you keep it inside.

No need to tell me the secrets of the Great pyramids.
Just tell me the ancient Egyptian word for getting high.

If you consider the fact that life on Earth is just a momentary vibration in the dissipating echo of the Big Bang, silence don't seem so golden...do it?

Hating the government has become so popular
scoundrels are virtually assured of election.

Childhood illusions are only surpassed by those of the intelligentsia.

T.S. Elliot said that, "Bad writers borrow and good writers steal."
Did he say that before or after he got caught?

Like politicians and actors, lovers are cherished for their ability to make us believe what we know to be false.

Even the virtue of moderation can sometimes be extreme, dangerous and completely irrational.

Compassion: The ability to feel what you don't feel.

Despair: Suddenly realizing that the light at the end of the tunnel is just a reflection from your flashlight.

One's man's ceiling is another man's floor: legal terminology which means that when the plumbing leaks, both will have to share the mopping chores.

Life: Postponement of the inevitable.

If walls could talk . . . we wouldn't have to telephone our neighbors.

The ability to accept criticism can lead to self-doubt or self-respect
depending on how you use your time.

Your mind is not your personal property …regardless of what you think.

"The early bird catches the worm": Warning that you should sleep a little longer until they start serving something decent for breakfast.

The ability to make others laugh is the only form of power that should be abused.

Forgive and forget . . . so that later on you can do the same.

The roller-coaster ride: A voluntary experiment in which participants attempt to transfer mental illness to the body.

East is East and West is West, but any roadmap will easily convince you otherwise.

The good lord gave us free will . . . the devil then countered with advertising.

Light is the only metaphor that should be taken literally.

Autobiography: Fear of long-term memory loss.

When mortal enemies find common ground it usually means that they've agreed on their choice of cemeteries.

Crocodiles cry…so do clowns…deceiving lovers too.
Almost makes you appreciate the sheer genuineness of onion tears.

They always drink the same thing and never pay. They always drink alone and never tip. No wonder we consider the action of the mosquito repellent.

Insomnia: When your mind refuses to stop working while it seems as though
Your dreams have gone on strike.

People prone to guilty fingers try to keep 'em clean by putting them on a preaching hand.

In the geometry of Life most vertical lines end up crooked.

Embrace your fear with a lover's passion and the femme fatale will leave you.

Live life on the edge if you can't make heads or tails of it.

Of all those who claim that they love people, the most believable is the cannibal.

Human body: The bread of life destined to become stale.

Even the most popular person in the world must dance to the last song without a partner.

The gifted can do much more than simply open the present.

For the writer…manual labor means *grasping* for thoughts and *squeezing* the meaning out of words.

In a calculated risk, you have to consider all the plusses and minuses if you want to figure out the aftermath.

Some holy men have my deepest respect. Takes a lot of pride to think you're not human.

Regret is the echoing scream eternally silent in a dead man's dream

The "anti-toast": Glory to the pagan…to the irrational animal soul
And may the gods have mercy on the cruelly civilized mind.

Mid-life Crisis: Period of life when most men experience their first sexual feelings for the very last time.

Prestige: Top-dog status for the underdog.

The door to the past can only be unlocked by the keys of a fool.

Desperation: An urgent need to wish in "fast forward."

Social inequality will not be changed by politics or economics. For the elite are obliged to be exclusive by definition. First, shoot all the linguists!

Hesitation: When desire and the will haven't been properly introduced.

Flattery: The antidote to unwelcomed persuasion.

Fashion conscious: when one's Ego is woven into the fabric of their clothes.

Self-knowledge: A sly wink from your third eye.

The cockroach does not drink or smoke nor swear loudly and over-consume your food. He does not snore or steal your money and will never try to seduce your wife. Yet this ideal house guest still manages to embarrass you in front of family and friends.

Creative writing: Defiantly building another tower to transcend the limitations of language.

Consider the circle . . . accused of abetting witchcraft, associated with flawed reasoning, even branded as vicious. Are we not simply jealous of the circle because it is so well-rounded?

Art imitates life . . . except where prohibited by law.

Theory: Using the power of the mind to comprehend something which the mind has been powerless to comprehend.

Pity the hapless pauper who lives his entire life on handouts until charity provides one final insult: The coffin- an unwanted gift that cannot be returned.

Women often complain about men which only makes men complain about women,
But then again…who's really complaining?

Whoever said, "Man ultimately kills that which he loves" must have been a florist.

Computers are an extension of the brain, but for some- a prosthetic device.

Feelings present an obstacle to clear, rational thinking, but in our search for the truth we manage to find a way around them.

Variety is the spice of life but if most people are content with plain old salt and pepper my advice is to go with the pepper. Pass the salt.

The aim of poetry is to outshine the sun, overcome death, and assist in seduction. Poets fail miserably at reaching all these goals, but one out of three ain't bad.

Suspicion is the front door to the Devil's house.

If change is permanent, we will meet again. And again.

The first shall be last and the last shall be first.
But I'm still not giving up my place in line.

Whoever said little girls are sugar and spice and everything nice probably never changed a diaper.

"Curiosity killed the cat."
The mouse that put out the poison is innocent of all charges.

Revenge is sweet, but a good Christian is always on a diet.

Last night I dreamed of a camel passing through the eye of a needle.
And he did it without even lifting his leg.

Master: Remember . . . the *Good* go to Heaven, the *Bad* go to Hell
Pupil: That I understand sir, but where do people go?

Jealousy in romance is the voyeurism of self-punishment.

Reality is a hyphen between two worlds.

The bard perceived the entire world as a stage because we all do. Drawn by the colored lights, no doubt, we linger long and only the few seek a quick exit. Itinerant puppets wearied of the playwright's string; they hope never again to have to wait in the wings.

Just when you think you've got it made, you wish you could make it all over again.

Journalists strive to be objective.
Remarkably some try even after they've been hired.

When a student oversimplifies the complex, he gets an "F."
When a professor does it, he gets recognition.

Flying saucers are real. The people who see them are not.

If you've been there, seen everything before and heard it all before,
You may as well work on weekends.

Follow your heart, but keep some distance.

Without imagination nothing would seem real.

When the curtain comes down…at least put on some underwear.

Books contain knowledge in order to prevent it from possibly contaminating the populace.

If you fail to study geography, you'll probably think the Antarctic was a pesticide used by Noah

The devil ain't nothin but negative ideas. Take away all the negative ideas in the world and all you got left is God – the big Yes.

As you get older and more mature…you stop making foolish mistakes. Then you live to regret it.

Punishment is pre-meditated, but crime can be accidental. Virtue is usually both.

All the world's a stage…and who can deny that even the well-paid players perform for one reason and one reason alone: To make you, as well as themselves, think that what comes before the fall of the curtain is more dramatic than the critical silence that follows our self-conscious applause.

After three thousand years of persistent inquiry, it is rumored that Philosophers now know the meaning of life…okay…who blabbed?

History is the mess left behind by uninvited guests.

Romanticism is a rebellious shadow trying to outrun the rays of the sun.

When there is peace on Earth, war will suddenly become a human right.

Mysticism is the cloud behind the sun.

Kissing your sister is different from kissing your lover. But let's not discuss it further if it's all the same to you.

A writer does not create. That would be plagiary.

Depression is an intermission in the game of illusion.

Hollywood directors are the trash collectors of culture. And the producers just keep piling it on.

If you've been around the block a few times you know that death is right around the corner.

The historical utterance "Give me liberty or give me death" is very useful in instructing young citizens. It teaches them never to limit their options.

There are no atheists in a fox hole cause they're usually not dumb enough to join the military.

For the eternal pessimist, optimism is a once in a lifetime opportunity

Promises were made to be broken so that promises would be able to mend

Chastity ends when the music begins

Never talk to strangers…and you'll never have a friend

Compassion is the make-up of the spiritually vain

Forget your foolish pride…and you'll end up a humble servant

The amount of stress you feel is inversely proportional to your IQ

Courage turned to Fear when it unexpectedly looked in the mirror

If you only live once then do so…by all means

Fools argue among themselves. Enlightened scholars debate each other.
The truly wise just play music

Intuition is weak perception suffering from delusions of grandeur

Flying is a way of laughing at the Earth. But you know who gets the last laugh

Bartenders are character witnesses to the assassination of your respectability by your own hand

The message of the first raindrop bears repeating

Spring is conception, summer is birth and the body is the autumn deception of existence.

The will to change is determined by a chance to forget.

Personality is a game of musical chairs. Hypocrisy occurs when two are caught sitting in the same seat.

A cynic is someone looking over his shoulder at the future.

A smart writer wakes up before his imagination does so he can hear it talking in its sleep.

The cemetery is a place to briefly visit those who used to briefly visit those who used to briefly visit.

For a man, possessive love is the strangle-hold of a headless horseman who's lost his grip.

The craving for revenge can only be satisfied by a flirtatious enticement of injustice.

Anxiety is an inarticulate beggar.

Never respect a "perhaps" or a "maybe" – they are merely the puppets of possibility.

Gaining wisdom means that you can ignore advice and disregard criticism
now that you know others are just as stupid as you.

Getting married is a nervous theatrical moment even though you both know the script and all the cues. Perhaps it's due to all those critics in attendance.

Secrets are little stones that are much too heavy to carry alone.

Advice to schoolteachers: Don't get upset when pupils lose their concentration in Friday classes . . . after all . . . day dreaming is what the elderly week does.

A penny for your thoughts . . . you're a millionaire!

There's a story on the white pages of winter's dark book, of a snowflake that falls careless and free until it settles down to wait for the light of dissolution that unites.

I thought at one time that asceticism was my true calling . . .
But it was just an echo of spiritual narcissism.

Colors are the candies and flowers in the romance between light and dark.

My bedroom ashtray was an invitation to smoke and I RSVP'd with a hot flame.

In the world of entertainment many performers work for peanuts
Exotic dancers are an exception . . . they perform for chestnuts.

The genius writes with a microscope what can only be read with a telescope.

Astronomy owes much to the reflective powers of the simple mirror which-when gazed into-always reveals the center of the universe.

Hindsight is just an oversight of foresight.

Was Scrooge the only psychologist to point out that the annual visit of Santa Claus is a guilt trip?

In the illness of life, pleasure is an attempt to treat the past and prevent the future.

Justice for all: Love is irrational – laws are not.

The eyes are the window to the soul, but most of us have the shades drawn.

For some . . . being guilty means that every now and then happens too often.

Sarcasm is the art of the boomerang compliment.

The Tao of Tyranny: The best way to control . . . is to give the masses complete liberty
so they may freely enslave themselves.

You're tired of being stepped on, tugged this way and that, so much that you feel you're going to snap . . . checked on to see if you measure up . . . knowing that if you don't, you'll be instantly replaced. No wonder–my little shoelace–you are fit to be tied.

You say the Blues make you feel good about feeling bad?
Well . . . and you thought you weren't religious.

Scientists insist on communicating with animals through the language of stimulus/response. The average pet owner knows instinctively how primitive this is.

Spirituality based upon Reason is superior because you get to pity others you *think* are morally inferior to you.

Dreams are the mirrors which reflect the images our minds must distort
to keep us asleep.

Faith is the sound of a broken clock still ticking.

Consciousness is a dance between yesterday and tomorrow
Insanity occurs when they both try to lead.

The Believer drives down the road of Life seeing a cul-de-sac
while fully expecting a detour.

When the expression "you have an interesting mind" becomes
redundant
human evolution will finally be complete.

Secrets, Mysteries and Magic: A Personal Journey through Speculative Freemasonry and Beyond (A Memoir which is 99% true…)

Episode I

1986: The Black Metal Box: a burglary that was not a burglary

My journey into the labyrinth of mystery, secrets and magic was triggered by a highly unusual event in my life - a burglary that was not a burglary. It was a break-in that occurred in my Chicago apartment that I shared with a commercial artist - Kevin - who owned a sophisticated camera plus very expensive equipment related to his trade. None of these were stolen. Likewise, my stereo and TV remained intact. Absolutely nothing of value was taken. Except for the one item treasured by the man who stole it - a card that he gave to me in a bar one night as we discussed the imminent demise of the Soviet Union and what the future had in store.

The bar was situated around the corner from where I performed on stage at the "Chicago Repertory Theater." The individual in question was introduced to me as a "pure Marxist" by a local college professor also in the bar at the time. Having just spent two years as a card- carrying member of the Communist Party of the United States of America, I was more than curious to meet and talk to this young man. His name - if it really was his real name - was Alexander. In his thirties I guessed. Alexander spoke flawless English with just a slight hint of a Russian accent. He was extremely concerned about the future of the communist movement and the current crisis in his country - the Soviet Union. Alexander told me he had obtained a Visa to emigrate to America by lying to the authorities claiming he was one among many Russian Jews discriminated against and persecuted by the system in the USSR. After about an hour of socialist discourse he handed me his "calling card" across the table and I looked in astonishment at what appeared there. Below his name was the image of a pyramid with a small leafy branch sticking out from underneath. Having studied Philosophy, Art and Literature I took this to symbolize humankind's mastery over Nature. Interestingly, the pyramid had no "all seeing eye" and was not truncated. However, when I flipped the card over there was printed one startling phrase on the back: "Light and Happiness for All People".

Why was he giving me this card? What was he thinking?

I nodded, slipped the card in my shirt pocket and continued with the conversation as if nothing had happened. The night ended on a pleasant note as we bid each other farewell and mentioned meeting again sometime. When I got home that night, I tucked the card away in my black metal box containing "valuable papers and documents" such as my original birth certificate and social security card. I honestly forgot all about it - as well as Alexander- until the break in. On the morning of the "burglary" that was not a burglary I noticed a man loitering close-by my apartment building. He looked vaguely familiar, but I was late for my class at the local university, so I did not have time to ascertain his exact identity or if - in fact- I knew him from somewhere. When I returned later in the afternoon, I immediately noticed the back window of my first-floor apartment had been tampered with. Reaching my bedroom, I saw that it had been ransacked, drawers opened, clothes strewn about and everything upturned. In the midst of the chaos was my metal box clearly open. I approached it slowly with a feeling of unease. Having one's apartment broken into is somewhat traumatic and the victim always feels violated. Realizing that something inside the metal box was the cause of all this made me feel "creeped out" and anxious. Within seconds of checking its contents I came to the bizarre and unmistakable conclusion that the entire purpose of the home invasion and "burglary" was so Alexander could retrieve that important card. It was very unnerving yet fascinating at the same time. Alexander did not know where I lived, did not know my phone number and I never told him my last name. Nonetheless he discovered precisely where I was living at the time. Why would this "pure Marxist" from the Soviet Union come to my apartment a full year after I had met him just to collect a card with a pyramid and a fictitious Jewish surname on it? I was more than curious...I decided I was now going to discover the meaning of this enigmatic episode. It would involve connecting some significant dots. Beginning, of course, with Freemasonry. Be aware, however, that these dots are not connected through a linear progression. There will be lots of back and forth movement as dots connect from the present to the past and back again. It is afterall a labyrinth we're talking about.

Episode II

1976: A Touchdown that was not a Touchdown. And an Inside Joke.

When I was young, I had heard mention of Freemasonry on a few occasions, but never gave it much thought. Just another fraternal organization that people join for comradery and perhaps a bit of networking. Weren't there half a dozen such groups in America? The Lions Club, Rotary Club, Kuwanis, Knights of Columbus. No big deal. But then I began to remember some strange moments in my life that made me wonder about the workings of this secretive organization. I didn't have to look far.

My best friend for more than a decade was a Mason and I never knew it. Until I put 3 and 3 together (Numbers will turn out to be significant). My good friend Mike was "different". Very open-minded. And funny as hell. He was the jokester and the trickster who turned everything into a game. But one time he turned deadly serious.

In our college days, Mike, myself and three other students were headed down South for a Bob Dylan concert - the Rolling Thunder Revue (where Joan Baez came on stage and sang "The Night They Drove old Dixie Down" and had the Southern audience in tears). But I'm getting ahead of myself. All of us were packed into a VW microbus - a vehicle that broke down halfway to our destination somewhere in Virginia. Mike brought his VW into a small-town service station to have it fixed. Or so he thought. A few miles down the road the VW conked out. I could see that Mike was exasperated and quite agitated. I guessed he was low on money at this point. After a few minutes of looking like Rodin's sculpture "the Thinker" he became animated and screamed " Fuck! Fuck! Fuck!". Then suddenly he made what seemed like a grave decision. In a very imperious tone, he ordered us all to keep our eyes straight ahead. No one was allowed to turn around and look back. As if we were leaving Sodom itself. He exited the vehicle and strode towards the intersection behind us. Everyone in the microbus complied with his orders as if hypnotized. Except me. I was always stubborn and willful. I looked in the rear-view mirror and saw Mike lift his arms up as if signaling a touchdown being scored. Literally within seconds a car stopped, and I could see Mike leaning through the car window talking to the driver. Five minutes later we were in some stranger's home garage where our savior spent half an hour *really* fixing Mike's VW. I learned later on through a bit of detective work in the library that Mike's "touchdown" gesture was in fact the international distress signal used by Mason's in need of help. I never mentioned to Mike that I had discovered this because I thought it too sensitive. If he were to bring up the episode, I would tell him the truth, but the incident would always remain buried and forgotten. The day after the concert we stayed on to explore the city. Mike insisted we all go to a Drive-in movie later on. Even though the AC in the VW was non-functioning, and it was ninety-five degrees at 8 PM, we all headed out to the Drive-in after an Epicurean stop at KFC. The heat was oppressive and the mosquitoes unbearable, but we all sat through a film entitled "The Man Who Would Be King" with Sean Connery.

When we arrived back home to Albany, I paid a visit to the library to pursue knowledge and truth. What I discovered was that the film was based upon a short story by Rudyard Kipling about what else? Freemasonry. Kipling also wrote a novel involving Freemasonry entitled "Kim" where a character refers to the local Masonic lodge as "the House of Magic". Interestingly, there was a famous British intellectual who defected to the Soviet Union and became a big KGB official. His name was Kim Philby. Coincidence? Or dot connected? In addition, I now understood why Mike always disappeared mysteriously on Friday afternoons and later re-appeared around 6 PM. That's the time period when Masonic lodges have their meetings.

"Weirdness Doth Pervade"

Then came Charlie Manson. For those who don't know...Manson was the leader of a Cult in Southern California and in the summer of '69 Charlie had ordered (hypnotized?) a number of his devoted followers to murder Sharon Tate - the rising star and pregnant wife of Roman Polanski. My friend Mike

- always the non-conformist- was fascinated by Manson and seemingly believed Charlie had magical powers (Manson supposedly made the prosecuting attorney Vincent Bugliosi's watch stop during his murder trial).

On one Friday night I paid a visit to Mike and he was deep in thought. I asked him why he seemed so contemplative. He proceeded to offer an explanation -if not justification - for the Manson family's action - portraying the gruesome murder of Sharon Tate as a good thing. He didn't seem utterly convinced by his own argument though. It was as if he were conducting some sort of thought experiment using fundamental rules of logic. "There are cultures in the world that see life as supreme suffering and view death as a welcome release followed by Eternal Happiness. Charlie said that Sharon Tate was so beautiful, she deserved to die. Maybe this is what he meant."

A few days after this discussion I hit the library again. I was slowly, but surely educating myself on "Speculative Freemasonry 101". What I next discovered is that the highest "virtue" of Freemasonry is referred to as "Love of Death". Was this another dot? Or just a tenuous thread of my own making? Then I read about the traditional Masonic Motto - "Momento Mori" - "Remember Death". Something clicked.

I had always been fortunate with regard to memory retention. Seems to be a family trait. In any event, I retrieved from my personal historical vault a moment of confusion that struck me as odd during the time. It was - I think - the mid 1960s. The comedian Morey Amsterdam appeared on the old Ed Sullivan show doing a stand-up routine. Very entertaining indeed. But when he finished his performance he waived "good-bye" to the audience and called out, "Remember Morey!" Many of the men in the audience laughed appreciatively. But only the men. I thought it was weird because it wasn't really funny. But I wasn't a Mason. Small dot connected, but a dot nonetheless.

Episode III

"Angel, Witch or Extra-Terrestrial?"
Moscow, Russia: 2004

Everyone called him Abed - a nickname for a rather long Muslim appellation denoting upper-class status. Abed was a student of mine and had become one of my best friends. His family lived in Damascus, Syria and his father was a prominent Mason. We had many shared interests: Smoking weed, astro-physics, astronomy and mysticism. During one of our "sessions" Abed began talking about "Red Mercury" and "Jinns". He told me of an incident with a friend in the Middle East involving this expensive substance - Red Mercury- and how when imbibed allows one to conure up Jinns - those naughty entities from "the spirit world" who have the power to grant your wishes. "They are mentioned in the Koran", he tells me. I would - like any rational, well-educated person - dismiss such fantastical nonsense, but my memory intrudes once again bringing me back in time to 1972.

I was an undergrad student at SUNY Albany (a god-awful place that I hated and couldn't wait to graduate from). My father had arranged for me to join a band called the "R & O Trio". This group consisted of two sisters - one on accordion and one on organ plus yours truly on drums and lead vocals. We were professional and popular in the area playing weddings, anniversaries, local hotel lounges and Moose Lodges. As it turns out Moose lodges are connected to Freemasonry in a kind of indirect way, being sort of a subsidiary. There is some overlap, however, and I experienced it big time one fateful night.

After having played at numerous Moose lodges we in the band knew pretty much what to expect. Until this one summer night. The girls usually just gave me directions to the next gig and I'd meet up with them there thirty minutes before starting time to set up. On this particular day, I was told to drive to their home in the country so I could follow their van to the lodge. Otherwise, I was told, I'd never find the place. They were right. Talk about a labyrinth.

When we finally arrived at the proper location what I saw shocked me. The architectural design of the building atop a hill was positively exquisite. One of the girls came out of the van, looked up at this wonder and exclaimed "This is a Moose lodge? Are you friggin kidding me? (She hated the actual "F" word and referred to those who use it too liberally as "F Troop"). Two men came bounding down the steep steps to carry our instruments for us. They seemed rather excited....as in "psyched!". Okay, we were good. But not **that** good. Why the hyper excitement? I wondered.

The hall of the lodge was quite modern with freshly polished hardwood floors. Very un-Moose like. In the middle was a long table covered with a white cotton cloth. In the middle of that was a silver fountain with ginger ale - I think - flowing down into the basin. That was different. But what really caught my eye were the fifty or so plastic cups arranged in rectangular fashion along the edges of the table. Inside each of them was a reddish liquid. While we were alone, our manager - the girls' father- explained to me that it was "Moose blood" and that it was sort of a tradition with this particular lodge to drink it at the start of the proceedings. He told me I didn't have to imbibe if I really didn't want to. Feeling my masculinity challenged I quickly grabbed a cup and downed it. And yes, I did need the ginger ale.

I remember setting up the drums, but after that everything was a blur and then non-existent. I can't remember a single song we played and as I said - I have a prodigious memory. What I do remember is driving home on my own along a dirt road with no van in sight. I looked up, as if hypnotized, at the full moon, as it rose higher and higher, the drummer boy smiling like a lunatic. A young lady appeared, an apparition at the side of the road hitch-hiking. As I slowed down to give her a lift, I could see she had an almost perfect figure. Hopping into my car she immediately sat sideways facing me. Absolutely beaming. I was quite taken aback as she seemed to devour me with her eyes. "Are you thinking what I think you're thinking? " was all I could say. She smiled, nodded her head, and said "Uh -huh". Suddenly I became paternalistic. To this day, I really don't know what came over me. Instead of taking advantage of the situation I quite uncharacteristically began to lecture her - gently- on how dangerous it was to be hitch-hiking on a country road at 3 o'clock on a Sunday morning. "Let me drive you home," I suggested. She paused for a moment - laughed - and then replied "Alright." Following her directions, I just seemed to get more lost so she suggested she drive since she knew the way. That's when the blurry feeling came back. I don't know how long it took, but the stars seemed to multiply as we got closer to her home. As she stopped the car, she turned to me and said, "I want you to meet my Mom". "Your Mom?" I replied incredulously. "Yes. Don't you think you could use a cup of coffee?" "Actually, that's not a bad idea", I said.

We entered her very modest home and I was promptly introduced to her mother - a woman of few words - but hospitable and kind. As donuts and coffee were placed on the table the young lady insisted that I tell her mother precisely what happened out on the dirt road and to include every aspect of our encounter. I was stunned. Why would I...? Why should I...? I mean it was awkward to say the least. I shook my head and said "Please I can't". "If you don't...I will" the girl responded. So I recounted the brief interaction in every detail - much to my surprise. Her mother nodded approvingly and then bid us both a good night.

The young lady said she thought it might be best for me to stay over since it was already past four. I decided that was a good idea because despite the coffee I was quite enervated. To my surprise she took me to her bedroom and undressed to her bra and panties. I stripped to my underwear as well. Now, feeling her warm beautiful body next to mine I had a sudden change of heart concerning my recently acquired paternal nature. I slipped my hand between her thighs and upwards. She gently pulled my hand back and away without saying a word and then kissed me - not on the lips, but on my chin. I felt a surge of pure love radiating throughout my entire being. Or so it seemed. The feeling was like nothing I had ever experienced. Was this magic? Who was this girl?

Feeling a bit guilty about my "faux pas" earlier I waited until I thought she was asleep, put on my clothes, left her house, and drove home as if in a dream. When I finally arrived, the sun was beginning to rise and feeling exhausted. I undressed, dropped my clothes on the carpet and plopped on the bed. When I awoke the next day, I picked up my pants and shirt and realized they were quite wet. I automatically smelled for traces of urine. Hey, who knows? But no. Just water. There was no cup or glass in sight and only my clothes were saturated. Not the floor, or wall, or bedside table. Now that's odd, I thought. But then what about the past night was not?

I still have no explanation for just about everything - including the missing five hours, but wait for the dot...

Years later, in 1992, I was a broadcast journalist in Moscow, Russia working at "Open Radio". We presented a two-hour English language program every day of the week from 7 until 9 AM. One morning my program director, Sergei, handed me the

latest copy of "The Economist" saying "Read the article about Russia". Towards the back of the magazine was an intriguing story about how a large amount of Red Mercury had been sold to America making some people in Russia loads of US dollars. This was the Economist mind you, not some wacky tabloid. "So it's real", I thought. "The substance exists!"
In between news segments we played a bit of music in order to give the listeners a break. I selected a tune by Queen - very popular in Russia at the time. As the lead singer belted out "Bohemian Rhapsody" I thought of his name. Instead of his real Middle Eastern name he chose to call himself "*Freddy Mercury*". Was this another inside joke? Was I experiencing synchronicity? Or just a strange coincidence?

Episode IV

"A Philosophical Analysis of the Elite and a visit to Guilder's Hollow"

Mana:noun
1. A supernatural force believed to dwell in a person or sacred object.
2. Power; authority.

How does one become "top dog" in society? Or is social status pre-determined?
Some say it's all about the "Promethean Figure" - one who through sheer strength of will and unbridled ambition takes his or her place as the most powerful because they have the "Promethean fire." We all have it to some extent, but the great ones have it in abundance -having more strength of Will than any other mortal. Anthropologists would recognize this as "mana," that special energy, (perhaps magical), that gives one *power*. It is an energy force that has a strong effect on others, making them want to follow you and obey your commands. If you're a film buff you may remember the ending of Spielberg's "ET" - where the alien says good-bye, touching the boy with his elongated finger and saying, "I'll be right *here,*" as a bright light of ET energy is transferred to the area corresponding to the third eye. This is ET performing the role of Prometheus. And it's quite Masonic I believe.

In Philosophy, another term for mana is "life-force". Those who prefer this term refer to the same phenomenon, but simply point out that not all people who possess a lot of mana become leaders. Some choose other paths: Artist, scientist, actor, business tycoon etc.

In Oriental philosophy this concept of mana or "life-force" figures prominently. In Hindu philosophy they speak of the seven chakras corresponding to where in your body this life force mostly resides. In Freemasonry, one may read about what members have called " the upward movement of the *inner-path*." Many actors - when speaking of the characters they portray - will make mention of where he or she is "centered". Same idea. Those who seek power are centered in one of the lowest chakras. But if one is even more willful, the energy rises up the *inner path* towards love and compassion, then creativity, and then wisdom. However, the highest level of life-force ascension is manifested around the top of the head depicted in religious paintings and icons by gold - an ancient symbol of spiritual perfection. Some would say that these spiritual masters are the true Promethean figures, the truly elite.

Rulers throughout history have possessed mana and have been careful not to lose it.

This explains "Royal Incest," the practice of marrying a close relative to keep the mana "in family." This may also explain why in powerful aristocratic families cousins have often married cousins. If you keep the mana "in family" you rule society. The problem is that Endogamy (in-breeding) results in biological degeneration. Off-spring will exhibit lower intelligence and physical abnormalities of a sometimes-freakish nature. It can also lead to health issues like hemophilia. An example of this biological degeneration involves the early Dutch in America.

In New Netherlands (now New York) wealthy Dutch aristocrats inter-married. According to legend, mutant off-spring were exiled internally to the upper regions of the Dutch colony far away from "the civilized world". Simply put...they were just dumped off far away hopefully never to be seen again. But I saw them!

"A Town full of Incest and Mana"

In 1976 I wrote a one-act play entitled "Persistent Visitor" which was presented at a local college in Albany, N.Y. One of the actors, Dan, became a good friend.
One evening after a performance Dan and I went out for a few beers at a local bar called "The Washington Tavern". While there the subject of Dutch aristocrats and their mutant off-spring came up. Dan turned to me and said that the descendants of the Dutch mutants still existed.
"No way!"
"No, really, they do."
He told me he grew up in Granville, New York not far from the Canadian border. Right next door to his hometown was a tiny place called "Guilder's Hollow." This is the location, he explained, where the descendants of the aristocrats were exiled to. Instead of dying off as expected, the early inbred Dutch survived and they themselves inter-married. So, if we focus strictly on mana, this would mean that the original internal exiles, though less intelligent and biologically inferior, still possessed the same amount of mana as their parents (thanks to Endogamy). This also meant that - because of continued in-breeding - a good number of descendants there probably still possessed large amounts of this life-force. Would they use it for good purposes or bad, I wondered?
The very next day Dan and I set off for Granville. He to visit his mother, me to visit you know who. I was not disappointed.
In order to observe a cross-section of Guilder Hollow's small population I decided that a local bar would be quite suitable. As I entered the tavern - the only bar in town - I imagined there was a sporting event on the television because I could hear the patrons urging on their team with enthusiastic fervor. But there was no game being televised. What the patrons were cheering about was a couple - probably cousins - who were openly copulating at the service area of the bar. She, with her legs in the air – and he, thrusting away to the rhythmic chanting of the crowd. I am no prude, but it was a bit too much for me. The locals were very animated and exuded extreme self-confidence. I felt intimidated by their vivacious behavior. After quickly downing a Canadian beer I left the bar satisfied I had seen proof of the legend - in graphic form. When I drove back to Granville

and the home of Dan's Mom, he asked me about my anthropological research. "How was the bar? Meet any mutants? What did you do there?"
"No. Just drank a beer and watched a show"
"Oh. Too bad. What were you watching?"
"All in the Family"

Episode V

"The life-force performs magic"

For better or worse I decided to become a professional stage actor in 1976. My first gig was in Albany, NY. At this time of my life my heart chakra opened up and I actually felt lighter. As if walking a few inches off the ground all the time. I also felt as though I had found my calling. I had talent! I was that good. Who was that amazing guy on stage? Certainly not me. My success gave me inspiration and ambition. I wanted more!
My good buddy in the cast was Frank. He played the part of King Henry the VIII. Damn good actor. I asked him one day: "Should I go to New York to make it?"
"No. Too much competition. You'll starve. Go to Chicago. I hear the theater scene is starting to flourish."
"Okay. O'Hare here I come."
Within a month I was living with my very rich Uncle in a gated community with guards and Japanese gardeners wandering about. He told me I could use his Cadillac whenever I wanted. I lived among 40 some-odd homes - all vacant while their owners were away in some exotic foreign location most of the year. My uncle himself announced that he would soon be vacationing in Europe for a month. But before that he wanted to make sure that I was "gainfully employed" and making some money to survive. Cheapskate.
He arranged to have me work in one of his cardboard factories, but first, he said, I would have to do an interview with the factory director - Jimmy Bob or something. A good ole boy. "Just a technicality" he assured me.
I arrived at the factory and met the director who escorted me to his office. He sat behind a big desk and leaned forward to question me.
"Paul Kindlon. Hmmm..."

"So, tell me...are you serious about cardboard?"
Somehow, I managed not to laugh. I really was a good actor.
While driving home to uncle's place I realized I would require entertainment while he was in Europe. Later on, I called Susan who had been in the show with me in Albany. She played the part of a wench. I asked her if she would like to join me and hang out for a while in style. She thought it was a great idea. The day after Uncle Ed left for Europe, she arrived. That's when the fun started.
One night we were smoking weed and watching a horror film. All I can remember is Bela Lugosi. I was pretty tired, so I told her I was "hitting the sack". She said she would join me soon, right after the film ended. I fell asleep almost immediately. Then I was dreaming. Bela Lugosi's character was approaching me menacingly. He was wearing white gloves that reached out to my throat to strangle me. I woke up punching Susan in the face. At that point I was propelled off the bed, vertically, about three or four feet. I hung there... still experiencing the fear that made me react so violently. Then suddenly I felt a profound and overwhelming sense of guilt and shame. Because I was levitating. I immediately fell to the bed like a rock. Susan, poor Susan lost it. She accused me of being possessed by the devil. (Never knew she was religious). The next morning, she was on a plane back to Memphis.
Levitating? Seriously?
I don't know how to explain it. Because it's inexplicable. I'm sure you don't believe it really happened. But - hey - neither do I.
By the way . . . if you're wondering how I was able to push my life-force all the way up to my heart chakra, here's the secret - I told it to go up.
You connect the dots.

Episode VI

"The Big Question"

I discovered that elite aristocrats in Russia did exactly the same thing with biologically freakish offspring that the Dutch had in New Netherlands. These unfortunate children were carted off to a remote area in Siberia where they were expected to die off in the harsh climate. However, they did not die off. Is it possible

they remembered why they were banished and abandoned and vowed
revenge on the royal family for allowing this practice to occur? Did the surviving members of this group select one man with the most "mana" who would be sent on a mission to infiltrate the inner circle of the Romanov family and destroy them? Was this one-man Rasputin?

Before Rasputin made his way to St. Petersburg he went on a journey – a spiritual quest. During part of this journey he spent 40 plus days in isolation and without food - far away from civilized life. Anthropologists call this the "Vision Quest". Stories abound about men who survived this "rite of passage" being able to perform magic afterwards. Indeed, according to Christians, Jesus Christ began performing miracles following 40 days without food and in isolation in the desert.

There are many instances of Rasputin performing what some might call "miracles" and he greatly impressed the monks he met with his life-force shining powerfully from his fiercely hypnotic eyes. It is said that Rasputin either struck you as a "holy man"(starets) or as "one possessed by demonic spirits". In any event, he got his big chance to enter the private world of the Romanovs when he was summoned on to care for Alexei, the hemophiliac son of Nicholas and Alexandra.

Using his healing powers, Rasputin seemed to cure Alexei's malady which, incidentally, was caused by too much in-breeding among the Romanovs. Having gained the trust and gratitude of Alexandra, Rasputin would graduate in time from a part-time spiritual advisor and personal healer to confidant and political advisor! His presence within the deeply religious family was seen as ruinous by many aristocrats close to the royal family and many citizens blamed Russia's ills on Rasputin. Prince Felix Yusupov and others would eventually assassinate this controversial "starets."

According to legend, his life force had become even stronger after the Vision Quest. So much so that Rasputin was not killed by the poison-laced wine they gave him or by the bullets pumped into his body three times at close range. His corpse-when it was eventually retrieved from the Neva River - revealed the cause of death to be drowning and that Rasputin had struggled to the last moment trying to break through the winter ice.

This story came full circle when I read about a certain Greet Hofmans who was a Dutch faith healer and "hand layer". For nine years she was a friend, confidante and advisor of Queen Juliana of the Netherlands, often residing at the palace. Like Rasputin, this healer deeply divided the Royal family causing enmity and conflict. Hofmans would have ended up like Rasputin, but left the Dutch royal court in 1956 after receiving a letter warning that both she and Queen Juliana's private secretary would be "assassinated if she did not leave "voluntarily."

Episode VII

"The Origins of Freemasonry in Russia"

By all accounts, Freemasonry in Russia dates back to 1731, when Captain John Phillips was appointed as the provincial grand master of Russia. Under the guidance of the "Royal Arch" in England, all Masonic activity in Russia was really organized by a "liaison" communicating instructions from this very elite lodge: his name was Anderson.

From the very beginning, only the best and the brightest were selected to become Russian Masons. At the time, that meant - of course- initiating aristocrats. The basic idea behind Freemasonry – the initiates were told - was to make "good men" even better so that the "good works" of these men would benefit society. However, shortly after the lodges in Russia were established a problem arose: the Russian Masons wanted to know the identity of the "Top Mason" in England giving out orders. All Anderson would tell them was that instructions came from "the unknown superior". Not recognizing that as a definitive and clear answer, the aristocrats became disillusioned and abandoned freemasonry. The early lodges simply closed down.

Interest in Freemasonry would return later on during the reign of Tsar Alexander I. Deeply spiritual and contemplative, Alexander enjoyed philosophizing with the exiled French senator, diplomat and scholar, Joseph de Maistre – a Jesuit-trained Scottish rite Mason. De Maistre was a mystical "spiritualist" and their very private talks about Freemasonry profoundly affected the impressionable Tsar.

When Alexander's troops triumphed over the Grand Armee of Napoleon and entered Paris in 1815, Alexander gave specific instructions to his officers to socialize with the French Masons there. What the Tsar did not know was that these particular French Masons were highly political - espousing liberal, anti-monarchist views and shouting "Liberty, Equality, Fraternity" while drinking with their new-found friends from abroad. Shortly after their return home, these very same Russian officers began planning an uprising against the Monarchy! Alexander I was no longer around, however, having been buried at the St Peter and Paul Cathedral. Some insisted he was still alive and had simply walked away from his "day job" to become a reclusive monk (Interestingly, Soviet authorities opened up his coffin in the 1920s only to find it empty).

The new Tsar - Nicholas I - would decisively crush this uprising on Senate Square in St Petersburg in 1825. The brave and idealistic rebels – now known collectively as the Decembrists- were almost all Masons dedicated to giving up their lives in order to light a "spark" and change society for the better.

The Russian poet and playwright Alexander Pushkin – also a Mason – did not manage to join the Decembrists in their quixotic adventure, but he was very sympathetic to the cause. He was certainly not alone in this regard. I specifically mention him here because eight years later Pushkin would write a short story entitled "the Queen of Spades". Critics to this day believe this to be a supernatural fantasy about avarice and gambling, but it is actually much more.

In reality, the "Queen of Spades" (later to become an Opera by Tchaikovsky) is a clever riddle in which the author reveals the "secret Masonic code" which is used to unlock the true meaning of sacred texts like the Bible and Koran.

While researching Russian Freemasonry as a graduate student oh so many years ago, I felt a powerful urge to find out the identity of that "Unknown Superior" mentioned earlier. "Why was Anderson so reluctant to divulge his name?"

I contacted the Scottish rite Masons in Chicago at the time and began visiting them at their local lodge adjacent to the Newberry Library. The brothers were quite affable and gregarious, but they themselves were unable to help me out in my search for the truth. Over time, I was finally introduced to someone who was considered an expert in Russian Freemasonry! I could feel that the Holy Grail was within my grasp.

I asked him – point blank- if it was possible to reveal to me the identity of the illusive and mysterious "unknown superior."

"Yes, oh yes", he replied, and then paused for a suspenseful moment... "You see…let me put it this way, it was either the Prince of Wales or … an extra-terrestrial. I will leave it up to you to decide which one to believe". That was not, of course, a definitive and clear answer. Was it perhaps another clever riddle? Dare I connect the dot?

Episode VIII

Cosmic Consciousness

Part 1- The Siberian Journey

During my first summer in Moscow I had an affair that later magically transformed into marriage. Her name was Julia and she arranged for us to take a trip up the Ob and Irtish rivers on a ship filled with tourists from Poland. Along the way we stopped at small towns and villages throughout Siberia - a stunningly beautiful part of Russia.

One of those stops was in the "Xanti" region where indigenous people live in Teepees like their ancestors who migrated to North America 30-40,000 years ago.

I was feeling under the weather when the ship dropped anchor, so Julia went out to explore on her own. When she returned she told me what she had experienced.

The local Xanti view Nature as a sacred Goddess. Geologists searching for oil, therefore, were "fair game". One had been killed just last year. The Xanti apparently had no history books or "Bible". She asked them how they accounted for their presence on Earth. Did they believe that God created them? "No", they replied, "our people were brought here on a space ship by superior beings from another part of the Cosmos." She also told me that the families survive by fishing and selling the catch to the local authorities. At the time (1992) there was a pernicious bacterium inside the fish they caught causing people to die rather young. The average age of death was thirty-two. Rather than being distraught by this fact, the locals rejoiced for they view life as supreme suffering and death as a great release into Eternal Bliss. Funerals were happy occasions where villagers celebrated the glorious "passing over."

The following year I began teaching at an American College in Moscow. During a Philosophy lecture on "Mysticism" I told this story because I found it fascinating. Afterwards, one of my students - a bit older than the rest - approached me to say something. She waited for the other students to leave the room and then informed me that her husband was a Cosmonaut. Moreover, her cosmonaut-husband had actually met an ET.

"Where?" I asked.

"In the anomalous zone out in Siberia." She paused and then asked, "Do you believe me?"

"I think I probably do," I replied. "There are many things which are seemingly 'unreal,' that cannot be explained."

Part 2 - "How many ETs can dance on the head of a pin?

Nikolai Fyodorovich Fyodorov. Most inhabitants of planet earth have never heard of the man, but they will eventually.

A polymath and deeply spiritual, this Russian philosopher and resident librarian at the Rumyantsev library had advanced cutting-edge knowledge in many of the hard sciences. Known for his humility and ascetic life-style (he mostly ate dark bread, drank only tea with an occasional slice of cheese and slept on an old chest instead of a bed), Fyodorov was practically idolized by some of the leading minds of the late 19th century. Dostoevsky, Soloviev, Berdyaev and Tolstoy were in awe of this visionary. And rightfully so.

Fyodorov "walked the walk", living his philosophy of life 24/7. Intentionally choosing poverty and chastity so he could focus entirely on knowledge acquisition, his words and actions were consistent, harmonious and always life-affirming.

Death, he said, is the true enemy and must be overcome. We should live forever. We should follow in Christ's footsteps and defeat death so that all of mankind will live in a heaven on earth. Sounded a lot like "Light and Happiness for All People" to me. Movements such as "futurism" and "cosmism" were directly influenced by Fyodorov's ideas.

For quite some time, of course, almost all scientists thought he was – well... bonkers. His reputation, however, is beginning to get a make-over because of wide-spread interest in the medical community on the hot topic of immortality.

After Fyodorov's death, a number of his followers gathered his notes and published a book entitled "The Resurrection Project". Here's a look at some of his main ideas . . .

Palingenesis: There is a genetic signature that remains in our bodies long after we die. We must - as a global community of loving souls - figure out a way to scientifically "resurrect" the bodies of our fathers, grandfathers and so on. Considered an absurd notion for more than a hundred years, some futurists are now enthusiastically working on this dream with serious research and experimentation.

On evolution: humankind evolved by force of will. We are bi-pedal not because our ancestors needed to "free up their hands" as Darwin believed, but because we "willed" ourselves to stand up-right. Anthropology has discredited Darwin's theory on bi-pedalism, incidentally. Our being, Fyodorov said, involves self-evolution as well as creating new external realities. Nature may have determined our biological make-up in the distant past, but now we are able to determine our own nature and create a new Nature. This notion foreshadowed the current trans-humanist movement by more than half a century.

Leo Tolstoy introduced Fyodorov to a very bright young man while at the library. Impressed by the boy's keen intellect, Fyodorov decided to take him on as a private student. The older scholar imbued and saturated the pupil's mind with ideas such as: we humans are spiritually repulsed by the harshness, baseness and violence of nature and seek to overcome that which pulls us down towards this baseness. Our aspiration as a species is to rise above the dirt and mud, away from the earth. This is why we willed ourselves to stand up-right and walk on two feet. This is why we built the pyramids and why we build tall skyscrapers - proof of our constant striving to rise above nature and its blind forces. In fact, if we could choose an image of humankind that expresses our true character, it would be a man standing on his toes reaching towards the stars.

By the way… the name of Fyodorov's private student? It was Konstantin Tsiolkovsky – the father of Soviet rocketry who once claimed in an interview that he "spoke to angels." Somehow, I believe him.

Episode IX

"Stupid Mouse!"

Every journey begins and ends in the imagination. Filtered through time and the emotional pauses of experience. Cleansed of all rational falsehood and meaning. This much have I learned and perhaps more. What I will never know is the why: that probing after-thought of jealous consciousness. Like a curious young boy left behind who insists on knowing the details of his older brother's dangerous exploits and manly adventures. The pleasure of memory robbed and replaced by a desperate yet harmless guessing game.

But my little mind wanders, I suppose.

Still in the labyrinth, I feel about with my extremities, aware of the sound of running, scratching and bumping into. The smell of my error in a bloody trail.

Wherever I go from here can only lead me away from the point of escape: that liberating space free from the search.

And so I remain. Lost and hungry.

When I had entered the labyrinth, my expectations were modest, but mine. Not borrowed beliefs accepted and projected as personal. That would be unwise.

Look!

Fire does not burn on a page inside a book. Skin is the only receptor of truth.

To learn is to feel and suffer. Your scream a philosophical utterance no one can refute.

Yet there are those who would turn away. Afraid to see the weltering proof.

Maybe courage is measured by the unsure moments we step-step forward. Into the unknown. Adding another layer to our incomplete being. Getting fat on life. Growing large and therefore unavoidable. A living presence.

As I prepare to turn another corner, I am hopeful still. I pray the right angle will lead me to something quite new. But if it doesn't, that's okay too. I realize this all must continue.

Why not?

Eventually, I will be plucked from the labyrinth by the scientist who put me here in the first place. To observe me try as he watches on with a cautious smile

Last Fox Trot in San Francisco
A Play in Three Acts

It is 1943. Eugene O'Neill and his wife Carlotta are living at Huntington Hotel in San Francisco's Nob Hill district.

Players:
Eugene O'Neill, who is now 55 years of age and beginning to suffer from neurological disease.
Carlotta Monterey, who is a rather imperious woman of aristocratic bearing and looks. A famous actress at one time, she is also 55 years of age
Myrtle Caldwell is a dear old friend to both Eugene and Carlotta. She is about the same age as them.
Jane Caldwell is the very young and beautiful daughter of Myrtle. She will fall hopelessly in love with the great playwright.
Kaye is the loyal house servant who has been with the O'Neill's for some time.

Act I
Scene One

Hotel room of the O'Neill's. It is a summer night. A fan is whirling. The telephone rings.

Carlotta: Yes hello? Excuse me. Stop…stop. I'm sorry did you not get instructions that Mr. O'Neill and I are not to be disturbed after ten o'clock? Yes, well it is now ten-thirty is it not? What? Who? Are you quite certain? …Well how do you know it's really her and not some prank or some nosey reporter? Indeed…I see. Hmmm… Hold on a moment, I'm not sure. (she turns to Eugene) Darling…it appears as though your loving daughter Ooona is on the line waiting. She says it is most urgent. Terribly important.

Eugene: Tell her to go to Hell. I'll pay for the ticket as long as it's one way.

Carlotta: Gene…what if she's serious?

Eugene: Serious is not a word that can be associated with that frivolous child in any way. What on earth could she want at this hour? Is she here in town?
Carlotta: For God's sake Gene. I'm not going to stand here all night holding the telephone. Do you wish to speak to her or not?

Eugene: Absolutely not. Why should I? She's a lazy, spoiled, vain little brat who doesn't know what she wants in life. One month a debutante, the next a model..and now I hear she wants to be an actress – not in some reputable theater – but over in Sodom and Gomorrah with all the pedophiles, perverts and drug addicts. And what disturbs me most of all is that she's trading on my name and reputation. Daddy – the famous American playwright, winner of the Nobel prize Her name is O'Neill so she must be special. But she's not accomplished anything on her own. I worked for my success…I worked hard to build the reputation I have. No one opened doors for me. I had to pry them open with these very hands every single day for years on end. It's simply not right that she should gain entrance with a free pass.

Carlotta: Good heavens man shut up. You're raving like a madman again.

Eugene: Don't tell me to shut up, Carlotta.

Carlotta: Someone has to. (she turns back to the phone) Alright then…yes, sorry for the delay. Mr. O'Neill cannot come to the phone just now, but you may tell Oona that if she wishes to speak with Mrs. O'Neill I am here at her pleasure. Yes, I'll wait.

Eugene: Did I tell you you could do that?

Carlotta: Since when did I ever need your permission silly Go make yourself a cup of tea and calm down before you have a seizure…yes? Oh, hello Oona. So nice to hear your voice. How are you? …I see. Well, that's a surprise. Quite unexpected. Of course, yes, (pause) Well I wish you both the best, naturally. No, your father is not feeling well actually. Don't worry though he'll be fine in a day or two I'm sure. Yes, yes, certainly I will. Thank you for notifying us before the papers come out with the news. What is that? Who? Louella you say...well that's certainly

better than Hedda Hopper. Indeed. Well, I really must go. Terribly good to hear from you. Yes, yes…good night. (She looks right at Eugene) She's eloped with Chaplin.
Eugene: (quietly raging, then bursting) Charlie??!! What about Salinger? I don't understand.

Carlotta: She's in love you idiot. Don't try to make sense of it.

Eugene: Oh I can make sense of it…even if you can't. Chaplin is my age. Figure it out. She has gotten married to her father because all her life he showed her no love. As a result she was searching for her father's love and finally found it in the arms of a genius. And she knows that I know this. That's what drives me mad.
She's playing a stupid game to hurt me and also prove that she's my equal. But she's played a foolish hand because I have the trump card. As of today I disown her. And she will be disinherited…of that you can be sure. (pause) I'm going for a swim. I need to think.

Carlotta: If that's how you feel.

Eugene: (leaving, he stops) Is that supposed to be a clever joke?

Carlotta: You tell me genius.

Act II
Scene One

Hotel room. There is a knock at the door.

Eugene: Coming! (he opens the door) Ah! Just a second (he counts out dollars and gives them to the young man) Thank you. (As Eugene is looking around the room for a hiding place, Carlotta arrives home)

Carlotta: Well…isn't this a pleasant surprise! Mr. O'Neill hitting the bottle behind my back. I'm sorry I returned so early and spoiled your little party.

Eugene: Don't be facetious, Carlotta. Show some kindness, please.

Carlotta: (mimicking an accent) "Is it kindness you'd be wantin, now is it?" Okay Gene…have it your way. You know how it goes, right? "I'll just have one drink." One becomes three which then becomes six and then you get so stupid you forget how to count. But who am I to interfere with a grown man's wants and needs? Just a once famous actress who gave up her career for you. Who sacrificed fame and success for a man who said he loved her.
A man who promised years ago – you remember that don't you? – promised he would never ever drink again. Are you not that man? Well if you're not (she takes a gun from her purse) Here…take this. Feel it. It's fully loaded. So if you are serious…really serious if you really want to commit suicide go ahead. But drinking yourself to death is such a long journey… take a short cut. Blast away!

Eugene: Don't talk like a fool.

Carlotta: Yes, you're right. It's better to act like one. Isn't it... Eugene?

Eugene: Eugene??!! Oh no…don't get crazy now. (she reaches for the gun) Carlotta…have you lost your senses? Please.

Carlotta…I haven't finished my best play.
(She stops momentarily and lowers the gun)

Carlotta: You….what a monster you are. My play! my play…my play! Your whole life consists of nothing more than soaking up all the pain you inflict on others so you may then squeeze it out onto the stage to torment the audience as well. It's nothing but a sado-masochistic talent masquerading as art, isn't it? Isn't it? Tell me!!

Eugene: Carlotta don't… (She takes aim and then shoots the bottle)
What the hell are you doing? This is not a theatrical play! That was very dangerous!

Carlotta: Of course it was. And if you're not careful you won't make it to the fourth act. The denouement may come early… What's wrong?

Eugene: It's my hand. My arm too.

Carlotta: Here sit down.. (he does) Gene you have to slow down, take a break…try to enjoy life.

Eugene: You know that's impossible.

Carlotta: Oh God Gene what am I to do with you. (she cradles his head in her arms) What am I to do?

Scene Two

Hotel room. Carlotta at the table. Eugene enters clearly in pain.

Eugene: Agh! I can't even type. My fingers hurt like hell and my arm is so weak.

Carlotta: Perhaps it's time you got a personal assistant.

Eugene: Damn it all. What the devil is wrong with me? I don't need this crap! Not now.

Carlotta: Don't be so stubborn, Gene. If your hand hurts and you cannot type or even write, use a secretary to do it for you.

Eugene: I don't need some complete stranger hearing my thoughts and feelings as they come out unfiltered. It would make me uncomfortable. Besides…it's too risky. How could I trust them to remain discreet?

Carlotta: Then we won't hire a stranger…we'll hire someone we both know.

Eugene: That might be even worse.

Carlotta: I have an idea actually. Do hear me out. (pause) I need to check, but we could probably obtain the services of Myrtle's daughter.

Eugene: But she's only a child!

Carlotta: She may not be a fully grown woman, but she's hardly a child anymore. Myrtle said that her daughter has completed finishing school and just arrived home yesterday.

Eugene: Little Janie?

Carlotta: Yes, Jane. Myrtle is very proud of her. She tells me her daughter is terribly bright and quite diligent.

Eugene: Eh! Never mind. It's a bad idea…bad idea.

Carlotta: Don't be so categorical and listen to me. I will call Myrtle and have her stop by the day after tomorrow with her daughter.. You can interview her and test her typing skills. If you do not like her for some reason- for any reason whatsoever – then we will put aside my idea and think of something else. We will find a solution. Don't worry. Meanwhile…let's try this. Who knows..you may find her both agreeable and helpful. If you don't do this for yourself at least do it for me so I don't have to listen to your moaning hour after hour.

Eugene: Okay, but the final decision is mine.

Carlotta: Of course, my love. It always is.

Act III
Scene One

Living room table with teapot and cups. Myrtle, Carlotta and Jane are seated. The radio is broadcasting news of the war. This goes on for a few minutes until Carlotta turns off the radio.

Myrtle: I don't think I can stand any more of this war business. It is so distressing.

Carlotta: I suppose we are lucky to be so far away from the brutal violence, but you have relatives in England. My heart goes out to you.
Myrtle: I worry constantly, it's true. I only wish it would come to an end quickly – and victoriously – for our boys.

Jane: Does anyone really win a war I wonder?

Carlotta: Yes, I can see your point.

Jane: Do you share your husband's position on Ireland remaining neutral, Mrs. O'Neill?

Myrtle: Jane dear, let's steer clear of politics shall we, please, and just enjoy this momentary respite from the madness. This tea is glorious is it not?

Jane: I was just wondering…it seems to me that the Irish are neutral because after hundreds of years of being oppressed and beaten down by the English they may be wondering if Ireland might not fair better under German governance.

Myrtle: Good heavens Jane!
(Eugene enters)

Eugene: Myrtle Caldwell how good to see you! This must be my little collaborator.

Carlotta: Yes, Gene…this is Jane who is ready and able I am told.

Eugene: My wife has explained to you your sacred duties, I suppose?

Jane: Yes, yes she has. I'm looking forward to assisting you.

Eugene: Good! We will begin the day after tomorrow. I start at nine A.M. and work until I get hungry. After that there is no set schedule as I work whenever the spirit moves me. Do you accept?
Jane: Aren't you going to test my skills?

Eugene: I almost forgot. (He goes to the player piano and music begins – Ain't Misbehavin' by Louis Armstrong) Do you fox trot?

Jane: (Getting up enthusiastically) Just watch me!
(The two dance rather well together until the song ends)
(Carlotta begins to applaud, followed by a hesitant Myrtle)

Myrtle: Well…wasn't that lovely?

Eugene: Excellent. I will see you in two days, Jane. Darling… I am going for a swim. Do enjoy your tea ladies…I had it shipped all the way from China. Myrtle…Miss Caldwell…till we meet again.

Myrtle: My my… he hasn't changed…That man lives to swim.

Carlotta: Yes, sometimes I wonder if he's human.

Jane: Me too. (pause) I'm sorry. I can't believe I just met the great genius playwright!

Carlotta: Why are you so surprised? He lives here. With me.

Scene Two

Same day. At the Caldwell residence.

Myrtle (entering the door): That was much too bold, Jane, much too bold. And what a performance you gave.

Jane: I was only enjoying myself. I was not acting mother.

Myrtle: I would rather hear that you were. Otherwise you are treading on very thin ice.

Jane: Oh, come mother…how could I not be charmed by such a man – he's an extraordinary artist…so kind, sincere and sensitive.

Myrtle: And married to a fine woman whom I've known for a long time. You have a number of suitors, Jane, why not give one of them a try?

Jane: Ugh! They are pygmies compared to Gene.

Myrtle Gene??!! Don't be so presumptuous. Is this the girl I raised?

Jane: I feel a connection to him somehow.

Myrtle: You hardly know him. For God's sake don't do anything foolish. That would be a tragedy…for everyone concerned. Consider my position Jane. Carlotta is already cross with me I'm afraid for not having prepared you properly. You are to type his manuscript and that is all. We do not need a scandal. (pause) Will you promise me that you will not use your feminine charms to entice him?

Jane: Mother…I promise I will not entice him, but I cannot predict what will happen if he entices me.

Myrtle: Your father will hear about this.

Jane: I have no doubt.

Myrtle: Such impudence. Go to your room please. And don't play those Jazz records so loudly. You know I'm not fond of that savage Negro music.

Jane: That is because you are not Dionysian. Like Eugene and I are.

Scene Three

Same living room table as first scene. Myrtle, Jane and Carlotta are seated. The house servant Kaye is pouring tea.
Carlotta: (to Kaye) Is Mr. O'Neill coming to join us?
Kaye: No Ma'am. He asked me to tell you he is quite anxious to get started with Miss Caldwell. And to send her into his office.

Carlotta: Right away?

Kaye: It seems so.

Myrtle: Well then Jane…it is time to get started. Remember what I told you. Keep quiet and do not interrupt Mr. O'Neill. Speak only when you are spoken to.

Carlotta: Good advice my dear. (to Jane) If my husband becomes annoyed don't take it personally. He can become quite fierce when it comes to social interaction. He is so used to working alone. Writing is such a solitary enterprise so it might be jarring for him at first, but I trust he will get accustomed to your presence.

Jane: I do hope so. (she rises and walks to the office) And I will do my utmost to please him I assure you. (she closes the door behind her) (Kaye looks somewhat shocked)

Carlotta: Bring us some more cakes and… (pause)

Kaye: Yes Ma'am?

Carlotta: Oh, nothing. Just the cakes thank you.

Kaye: Certainly Ma'am.

Carlotta: (looking up) Now how on earth did a fly get in here?

Myrtle: Oh Kaye!

Carlotta: Don't bother…I'll get it.
(she takes a nearby newspaper, smashes the offending insect and sits back down. There is an uneasy silence for a awhile)

Myrtle: So what sort of play has your husband produced this time?
Carlotta: It is a very sad tragedy.
(Jane can be heard giggling in the office. This continues for some time…).

Scene Four

One month later. At the Caldwell residence. Jane is at her make-up desk admiring a jade handle mirror that Eugene has given her. She sings a popular song entitled Dearly Beloved.

Jane: "Tell me that it's true, tell me you agree I was meant for you, you were meant for me.
Dearly beloved, how clearly I see Somewhere in Heaven you were fashioned for me.
Angel eyes knew you, angel voices led me to you.
Nothing could save me, fate gave me a sign I know that I'll be yours come shower or shine.
So, I say merely, dearly beloved be mine.
You were meant for me, I was meant for you.
Tell me you agree, tell me that it's true."

Jane then recites a poem he wrote to her:

Jane (Cont'd):"The magic of love was there. For me and you. Standing there. Blue coat, buttoned up to your chin. So beautiful there with the sea and sky in your eyes. And the sun and wind in your hair."

Jane laughs contentedly and looks in the mirror responding to imaginary reporters.

Jane (Cont'd): "Mrs. O'Neill…where do you and your husband plan on going for your honeymoon?"
I'm afraid that's a secret, gentlemen. I suppose we will put out a press release at some time.
"Mrs. O'Neill…where did Eugene propose to you?"
He proposed to me on our favorite stretch of beach as the sun was going down. Gene is such a romantic, really.
"Mrs. O'Neill…Jane if I may…some people are intrigued by the age difference between you and Mr. O'Neill. What would you like to say to those people?"
Well…like daughter like father I suppose. I'm sorry gentlemen, but I really do have a plane to catch. Eugene is waiting for my arrival. A few more photos? Very well, then, click away!

There is a knock on the door.

Jane: Yes?

Myrtle (entering): You are very pleased with yourself, aren't you?

Jane: I am pleased with life. I never thought I could be so happy.

Myrtle: I thought I had raised a daughter who would have a strong character. I see now that I have failed.

Jane: Yes, mother, I know that you are angry.

Myrtle: Oh no, I'm not really. Disappointed? Quite. Angry? Not anymore. This is the beginning of an important lesson you need to learn.

Jane: Is that what you call it now? A lesson?

Myrtle Yes Jane. You will learn – and fairly soon I suspect – that you do not really love Eugene. And that – in fact – he does not love you.

Jane: Ha! You are speaking nonsense.

Myrtle (picking up the Geisha mirror) Oh I'm sure it feels like love to you. It's wonderful. Believe me I know. But in time you will realize that you were in love with the feeling of being in love. You will also learn that Eugene is not in love with you, but with your young and beautiful body.

Jane: Stop it please! Why are you trying to make me feel bad?
Myrtle: I'm not. Not really. I know full well that in your current state you are incapable of thinking clearly. It's quite natural my dear. Enjoy your moment in the sun. (she hands the mirror back to Jane) But don't be surprised when you get burned by it. And you will.

Scene Five

Living room table with teapot and cups. Myrtle, Carlotta and Jane are seated.
The radio is broadcasting news of the war. Carlotta, Myrtle and Jane sit quietly listening. Carlotta gets up and turns the radio off.

Myrtle: How much more of this can we bear? On and on. It's endless. The death and suffering. It's hard to believe…here we are in the middle of the Twentieth century and we are still behaving like savages.

Carlotta is lost in thought.

Myrtle (continues…to Carlotta) Are you not tired of the conflict? (pause) Carlotta are you alright my dear?

Carlotta: Oh, sorry.

Myrtle: I said aren't you tired of the conflict?

Carlotta: (pause) Yes. Yes I am.

Myrtle I see well…Jane and I must be on our way. We have a golf tournament to attend. Our dear friend Helmsly will be there.

Jane: Hemsly . . . His name is Hemsly.

Myrtle: So it is. Well, thank you my dear for your kind hospitality once again. I do hope we will see each other soon.

Carlotta: Indeed. (To Myrtle) Dearest friend…allow me a moment with your beautiful daughter won't you?
Myrtle: Certainly.(she gets up to go)
Carlotta: Press my hands…dear. I will see you soon. God bless you. (they kiss. She turns to Jane) Just because my husband calls you Janie now do not be misled. No doubt you are harboring some romantic hope, but I assure you it is just an illusion. How do you see yourself Jane with regard to my husband?

Jane: The way I see it you are his Athena and he wishes for me to be his Aphrodite.

Carlotta: (laughing) You are a Janie come-lately. That's all you are.

Jane: Mrs. O'Neill. I understand my place. I know full well that you are and will always be his devoted wife.

Carlotta: Wife? If only…I am his nurse and his doctor, his protector and safe refuge, his solitary strength and soul.

Jane: But he does care for me.

Carlotta: Does he? Really? You are merely a palliative for a very sick man. Can't you see that?

Jane: I only see a genius.

Carlotta: And what do you ultimately want from this genius? That he will create a character based upon you? I suppose you keep a diary filled with all the words Eugene has uttered in your presence and that you've made note of every look and touch so that one day you too will become known. You can even get the diary published and make some good money…wouldn't that be nice?

Jane: I only want to be of service to the man who seems to need me now.

Carlotta: You don't understand. Not one bit. Eugene is in the final act of his life and you only serve as comic relief. Nothing more. It is the comedy of Oedipus meeting Electra and falling in love. How funny is that? At the end of the day you will be a fleeting moment of no significance. When biographers chronicle his extraordinary life I will fill up half the chapters whereas you will appear as a tiny footnote. Don't let that beautiful Geisha mirror fool you. Yes I know all about it. It was a birthday gift.

Jane: He also wrote me a poem.

Carlotta: (incredulous) A poem?

Jane: Yes…a love poem.

Carlotta: Unless you want to be pulverized and permanently disfigured I suggest you leave now. (she opens the door for her to leave) Oh…and if you ever show that poem to anyone, anywhere, for whatever reason… I will make sure that you will never want to look into that mirror ever again. Good night, dear.

Jane: But…

Carlotta: Leave!

She does so reluctantly.

Scene Six

Huntington Hotel. The Suite of the O'Neill's.

Carlotta: (Entering soaking wet) Look what you've done to me! Is this what you wanted? I tried to drown myself Gene! And wouldn't that be ironic? The only reason I didn't go through with it is because I realized you would win. After all, you thrive on the sufferings of those around you. You steal their pain for your plays and thus become famous by being a thief. Damn you!

Eugene: Let me start a fire…

Carlotta: This ends now. Do you hear me?

Eugene: I'm not sure I can comply with your desire.

Carlotta: I am not asking you a favor. I'm giving you an order.
Eugene: You know how well I respond to that sort of behavior.

Carlotta: You owe me your life you bastard. I've kept you sober for years. Not to mention my support and encouragement coaxing you onwards to create your finest works. That gives me the right to make demands.

Eugene: It simply grates. I have an anarchist heart and soul. Let us discuss this some other time…I'm not feeling well.

Carlotta: We are both suffering Gene. I'm exhausted as well. Do think of me just this once if you can.

Eugene: I try my love.

Carlotta: Not enough! Not as much as you should. Fire that girl now and I will shut up completely.

Eugene: I do not wish to do that.

Carlotta: I don't care! I'm going mad I tell you. You know how I am. There is a rising vortex of rage inside of me that I cannot suppress.

Eugene: Janie is good for me.

Carlotta: Well she is bad for me! Don't force me to do terrible things Eugene. You know I will.

Eugene: Don't threaten me.

Carlotta: I will threaten you until you come to your senses.

Eugene: You are going to drive me to drink again.

Carlotta: How dare you! You infuriate me! (She grabs a butcher knife. He quickly retrieves a pistol)
Eugene: It's loaded…don't move an inch.

Carlotta: Go ahead you misfit. You wouldn't survive a week without me. Damn you!

As she lunges, he flings the gun away and takes her by the neck. She digs into his hands with her nails. They are both screaming horribly.
Eugene pulls away and begins shuddering, his right hand shakes uncontrollably as he begins to cry. Carlotta embraces him in a motherly fashion.

Carlotta: I think you should rest now.

Eugene: Yes…I think I will. (He moves away still very much in pain.) And what will you do?

Carlotta: Love you, of course.

THE END

Galileo in Chains
A Play in One Act

Players:
Pope Urban VIII
Sister Maria Celeste
Galileo
Sister Luisa
Cardinal Richelieu
Mother Superior
Doctor Ronconi
Priest in black

Scene I

The residence of Galileo. There is a chair, a table, a fireplace, a bookshelf filled with manuscripts and a telescope near the window.

Cardinal Richelieu: Yes I believe. You, my friend, seem to think faith is a heavy burden- a weakness rather than a strength that supports and sustains the soul. Look at that ugly contraption! You have used your instrument as a weapon to attack Holy Scripture which clearly states that the Sun revolves around the Earth. You maintain against all common sense that the earth revolves around an unstable Sun. Any fool with two eyes can see how absurd that notion is every single day.

Galileo: Your Eminence…the naked eye is quite limited. My telescope enhances our perception of the world and therefore our knowledge.

Richelieu: Did the apple on the tree of knowledge enhance Adam's perception or make him blind to the wonders of Paradise? Do you blindly trust in every innovation that comes your way? Adam took a bite from that tempting fruit while it appears that you have swallowed it whole. Was your reckless behavior prompted by some evil influence one wonders. Or did you simply make an honest mistake? That is the question we must ponder and examine. I could easily say to the Cardinals that you are in league with the Devil who has used your telescope as a means of attacking the authority of the Church. Moreover, I could say that it is clear that you use this instrument of Satan to undermine the sacred word of God as it is manifested in Holy Scripture.

Galileo: The only league I know of is that league of pigeons who oppose me and want to silence me. You do know that the Pontiff supports me on this matter and has even looked through my telescope at the celestial bodies that God has placed far beyond our reach so that we need stretch ourselves beyond our bounded state in order to grow in our knowledge of this vast universe -whose immense beauty attests to the power, love and glory of the God who made it. Do not blame the Devil for your shortcomings for he is surely on your side in wanting to keep mankind dwelling in the darkness over which he presides. Rather than threaten me you should admit to the truth. Your dogmatic short-sightedness has been defeated by the far-sightedness of my telescope.
Richelieu: I will not respond to such a preposterous argument for it is beneath my station. I will only say that you are hopelessly lost… and suffering from the most serious of all sins – that of pride. I am here to help you Galileo. Why won't you listen to Reason?

Galileo: I would love to listen to Reason, but the man who could supply that uncommon commodity was burned at the stake by your Cardinals.

Richelieu: That is your uninformed opinion only. It was determined by consensus after much careful deliberation that Bruno was a heretic who conjured up the most absurd notions. An infinite universe. Form and matter united as something called "atoms". Pure madness.

Galileo: You dare speak of madness? Your Cardinals are obsessed with trying to divide nature into two philosophical categories, but the book of nature is written in the language of mathematics.

Richelieu: Future generations, I am sure, will see that the Cardinals were correct and posterity will vindicate them in the light of retrospection and increased knowledge. Galileo…

despite the cold reception you have given me I will try to save you mortal soul…despite your haughtiness and crude insults. I once again urge you to reconsider your position and give us some room for compromise. The Cardinals have instructed me to offer you a chance to avoid punishment. They are good and just men doing God's holy work for the benefit of all the faithful, including you. They admire you, you know, and they are extending a helping hand - please take it for it is a most generous gesture. You would be a fool to reject it. If not…well the truth is you may well be condemned… for this affair has grown large. There is now a powerful push by a wider circle of concerned notables unfavorable to you who are most difficult to resist. As a learned man of science you understand the phenomenon of momentum I am sure. But you can halt this rush to the abyss. At this critical point your fate is not going to be determined by us, but by you. Simply admit that what you propose concerning a heliocentric world is just a theory – nothing more. The Cardinals are not asking you to change your work – they may even help get it published.

Galileo: In Latin or in Italian?

Richelieu: Even in French if you wish. All we ask is that you change one simple word. Is that so difficult? Label your findings a theory and the majority of Cardinals will be satisfied. One word will not affect the body of your work. Be reasonable and take this under grave consideration. May God bless you and give you guidance.
(He exits)

Scene II

The Vatican

Richelieu: Your Holiness you must understand…if the masses are allowed to see the truth on this matter they will lose respect for the Church, but what is worse is that they will lose the fear of God. The future of mankind is at stake…for without a proper fear of God men will feel they can engage in all sorts of immoral behavior. The beastly passions within us will be released and chaos will prevail. The belief in a God of judgment and divine retribution acts as a break on man's bad intentions. Without it people will be tempted to carry out actions that satisfy our lowest impulses. There will be a preponderance of thievery, rape and murder and mankind will be plunged into darkness. This is why the masses must not be allowed to know the secrets of Galileo. We must safeguard civilization and the advances of Christendom.

Pope Urban: Perhaps mankind can benefit from these new findings. Why are you so pessimistic?

Richelieu: Your Holiness…I am a practical man. A realist. You and I and the Cardinals have an Empire to maintain that brings order and stability to the world. The Church is at the center of this world and it is indispensable. Over the centuries we have created a new world order. Without the Church and the central role that it plays, the world order would go spinning out of control. A new breed of Barbarian would arise along with witchcraft and pernicious paganism. Therefore, the Church must be vigilant and vigorously defended. We simply cannot afford the luxury of freedom of expression at this time. Perhaps in the future when mankind is ready and properly prepared for these new ideas it may be possible. But at this present time, we must firmly adhere to the tried and trusted ways that have served us so well. Galileo must carry his cross as Christ did.

Urban: Are we to crucify him then?

Richelieu: Not crucify, your Holiness. We will simply have him live a quiet life of seclusion. Not in prison, but at some ambassador's residence. You must understand…there are those among these very walls who have spoken of using fire to cleanse Galileo of his most grievous sins. And arranging for you to suddenly die in your sleep.

Urban: Have we come to that at last?

Richelieu: I'm afraid so. I'm sorry to say. But there is a way out as I say. You have an opportunity to save both Galileo and yourself. You must denounce him as a heretic. This is absolutely imperative and of primary importance. We must set an example.

Urban: Allow me to think this matter over. How much time do we have?

Richelieu: A day. Maybe two.

Urban: Leave me then. I shall call upon you with my decision.

Richelieu: May the Lord bless you and give you guidance.
(He exits)

Scene III

The residence of Galileo's house arrest.

Urban: Please forgive me my dearest friend. I felt there was no other recourse of action. The truth is I was put in an untenable position. An ultimatum was given to me by the Holy Office.
Galileo: I see. So the pursuit of science has been squashed by a small faction of Cardinals whose world has been turned upside-down by my proof and now they cling to their bibles like geckos attached to the ceiling. Believe me…I know that I have many enemies, but I also have friends. Clavius and all the Jesuit astronomers at the Collegio Romano are on my side. Descartes and the Rosicrucians support me as well. What you don't understand is that your victory is a temporary illusion because every attempt to silence and gag the tongue of truth is followed by a long-suppressed shout that echoes even louder throughout the ages.

Urban: We shall see.

Gal: Your Holiness I met with you six times and you made it clear to me that my ideas were not foreign to you. Indeed, you confessed to me that you share my conviction of a heliocentric world in which the sun is located at the centre of the revolutions of the heavenly orbs and does not change place.

Urban: That is true. But let us be honest. The masses are ignorant and weak-willed. We must protect them from themselves. I've come to realize that revealing the truth about the nature of the universe is a perilous exercise fraught with danger of the highest order.

Galileo: What you are saying is that we cannot share knowledge with the ignorant masses because they are dangerously uneducated yet how can they become educated if we fail to share knowledge with them? Do you agree with Cardinal Richelieu that my ideas will lead to atheism and chaos? Do you Maffeo?

Urban: I have come around to that point of view, yes.

Galileo: Oh dear…They have killed my old friend and replaced him with a marionette of whom they are the puppeteers. You think that not believing in God would result in widespread immorality and criminal behavior not ever acknowledging that there have been God-fearing men in the Vatican who have corrupted the Papal throne for hundreds of years…cavorting with harlots, stealing money and land, supporting mass murder in the Holy Land all in violation of God's commandments. You practice the logic of a school boy who has read too much Aristotle.

Urban: Do not judge me so harshly. I have endured many hardships over these many years. Like you I too am weary and suffer from many maladies. Your book is considered more of a danger to our religion than Luther and Calvin combined, and your teaching of the prohibited doctrine has not made my life very easy. Why did you forsake me? Am I really Simplicio? You must know that the Medici's want me gone. I've heard of a plot to poison me. The Spanish have a naval fleet ready to forcefully remove me from office at any moment. There are many who falsely accuse me of working for a foreign enemy. I feel I am caught in a web of deceit. (He starts to leave) I hope you do not find your living conditions too oppressive.

Galileo: Stop Maffeo! (pause) take a look through my telescope.

Urban: I haven't time.

Galileo: Maffeo…you were just as enthusiastic as I about astronomy and the telescope. What has happened?

Urban: I haven't the time. Or perhaps I am forced to look more closely at the reality nearby. I cannot afford to be a dreamer.

Galileo: I still dream…I dream of a world in which every man and woman will have a telescope to study the Heavens.

Urban: You are naïve my dear friend. Only a small number will make full use of its powers. The young will merely use it as a plaything. Adults will use it to secretly watch couples who are naked and copulating. And the elderly will be afraid to even touch it for fear that it may explode. I must go now.

Galileo: You think you have restricted my movement by confining me to house arrest, but I assure you…due to the rapid spinning of the planet I dwell on I am- right now - moving hundreds of times faster than your best horse-drawn carriage. And when I look through my telescope… I travel farther than a thousand Marco Polos. And yet I am in chains. Chains that shackle the spirit and prevent freedom of expression. The eyes of all Europe are upon us - waiting to see if the Vatican is open to unfettered scientific inquiry. Tell me Maffeo…without my voice who will speak for the stars? Who?

Urban: We must abide and submit to God's will. It is the only solution. Goodbye Galileo.
(He exits)

Scene IV

Sister Maria Celeste lies on her death bed. There is a priest in black near the bed performing last rites of Extreme Unction. Hovering over Maria Celeste are her doctor and sister Luisa.

Doctor Ronconi: Do you wish to pray?

Maria Celeste: (speaking slowly in between spasms of intense pain) What date is today?

Doctor: It is April the second dear child.

Maria Celeste: It is a full moon then. Please. Open the curtains so that I may see my old rival for my father's heart.

Doctor: Certainly.

Maria Celeste: The rose…

Doctor: Sister Luisa is coming with it quite soon. Some broth perhaps?

Maria Celeste: No need. Soon I will depart.

Sister Luisa enters with a rose and places it in Maria Celeste's hands. She takes it and writhes in pain, then calms down

Doctor: Does the rose comfort you? Do you want to pray?

Maria Celeste: Together with the rose… you will be able to accept the thorns… that represent the bitter suffering of our Lord… its green leaves symbolizing the hope… that we nurture of the reward that awaits us… after the brevity and darkness of the winter of the present life… when at last we will enter the eternal spring of Heaven… which blessed God grants us …by His mercy.

Sister Luisa: Such exquisite and sublime thoughts you have sister. You are a poet.

Maria Celeste: I am my father's daughter. (She experiences a final paroxysm and succumbs to eternal slumber)

Doctor: (Checking for signs of life) Poor girl. She didn't get a chance to pray.

Sister Luisa: Did you not hear?

Doctor: I must make arrangements. I will return shortly. (He exits and the Mother Superior comes rushing in)

Mother Superior: Where are they?

Sister Luisa: Where are what?

Mother Superior: The letters from her father!

Sister Luisa: In the cabinet.

Mother Superior: I must destroy those letters that Galileo sent to Sister Maria Celeste. Every single one.

Sister Luisa: But why? She is innocent and uninvolved in any of the outside conflicts that so excite and disturb the authorities.

Mother Superior: As long as her father is alive – merciful God protect him – we are all in grave danger. The fact of her innocence or even ours is irrelevant dear sister. For those whose hearts are darkened by bitter malice towards the illustrious one are so moved by a need for revenge that mere communication with him alone - for them - would amount to collusion and a guilt equivalent in nature to heresy as well as disloyalty to the Church. Dear Galileo is not being persecuted for simply looking at the heavens and calculating the movements of the planets. He has run afoul of the authorities for revealing secrets – secrets contained in these letters- that they do not want known to the larger public. Secrets that would harm their reputation, expose them as liars, and result in a lack of respect for authority. Galileo will not be the last man to be persecuted for revealing the truth. In future times another device of greater powers than the telescope will be invented, and some brave soul will use its powers to reveal an unpleasant truth that exposes the lies and hypocrisy of the leaders of that future time.

Sister Luisa: But surely the citizens will rise up to defend and support such a brave soul?

Mother Superior: I have no faith in that regard. The citizens are too easily convinced by sophists who can portray a good man as a danger to security or as working for some evil foreign power.

Sister Luisa: But what of the religious leaders? Would they not speak out?

Mother Superior: And jeopardize their luxurious lifestyles and splendid homes? We live on earth sister, not a heavenly star.

Sister Luisa: (forlornly) Yes…I know.

THE END

Alpha Male

A woman can only take so much. True, she knew when she made the decision to marry him
it was clear he was the playboy type. But Evelyn thought she could change him.
It was also true that her marriage was actually pretty good. Except for the affairs.
By divorcing him she would be giving up a lot. His friends and associates would all shun her.
The fine ladies of society would practically disappear. For a variety of reasons.
She would miss the mansion of course. It had become home. The servants would stay with him,
but that did not matter. Of all of them she really only liked Pierre.
Carrying on with that dense widow from London did not upset her that much. For many reasons.
Besides, she knew he would grow tired of the boring baroness quickly. Which he did.
She also didn't mind that fling with the politician's wife – what's her name. An ugly little
duckling with no charm or class.
But this time Wellington had gone too far. A certain tacit agreement between them had been
broken. And to break it by having a series of romps with a frivolous, silly actress is simply too
much.
Evelyn was ready to confront him. Over dinner.
"You failed me." She suddenly blurted out over oysters.
"What now, my dear."
"Save the 'my dears' for your thespian trollope.
"Oh I see. Is this jealousy or something else? "
"Both. I'm giving you an ultimatum. Leave her immediately or face the prospect of divorce and
public shame."
She knew that this was his Achilles heel.
"You dare threaten me? Are you not aware of your place and role in this relationship? "
"Fully."
"Then why do you insist on committing social suicide?"

"It's a matter of dignity."
"Look at me you fool. And stop starring at your wine glass. Good. Now…look around.
At the opulence. The power. The glory. You my dear will lose so much."
"Are you prepared to be publically humiliated by me exposing your sordid affair with this
Hollywood bimbo?"
"Will not happen. I will hire a young man to testify that he had a lusty affair with you before
I even began dating my inamorata. I will also get one of my servants to testify that he saw you in
this man's arms. Now come to your senses. There is no need for drama. "
"You give me no choice, then." She stabbed her fork and knife into the fumed oak table and
began to leave.
"Wait! I swear that if you choose to go down this path I will crush you. Think!."
She did not.
As he had threatened and promised Pierre was called upon as a witness that Evelyn Magnus had
engaged in a love affair. To everyone's surprise, however, he testified that he was ignorant of
any such thing.
The next witness – Chester Dunstan – testified that Mr. Magnus had paid him to lie about having
an affair with his wife for a reward of one hundred thousand dollars. His testimony was
absolutely crucial.
In the end, Wellington Magnus III was humiliated socially and on a personal level.
Sometime after the proceedings, Evelyn managed to meet with this Chester to find out why
he had testified against her husband.
"When I found out how much money the dude really has I was pissed – I mean really angry –
that he disssed me by offering a hundred thou. This way I'm getting a lot more because I got a
little secret up my sleeve. The thing is…I got pictures of your husband with Pierre."

"Pretty Pierre?"
"Yep. Pretty smart Pierre as it turns out."
"Do tell."

End of the Class

"However, as we can see here…Zero divided by Infinity equals…. Zero!"

"Oh my God, no way! Sir?"

"Yes Crawford. What is it now?"

"I mean…how can you be so sure? Can we maybe discuss Infinity conceptually?"

"Conceptually?"

"Yes. I just see this as being problematic, sir."

"In what way, pray tell?"

"Well…you mentioned before that any line segment – let's say A to B – can be divided by two like…forever! Doesn't that mean there are an infinite number of points between A and B?"

"Yes, of course."

"But don't you see? That means if you go from A to B you must travel an infinite number of points in a finite amount of time. Which is impossible. So, either motion is an illusion or mathematics is . . .

"Crawford…the subject of this class is mathematics, not philosophy. If you concentrated more on the former rather than the latter, perhaps you would not have a C average at this time."

The other students laughed. Like…all of them.

Crawford was not angry, He came to class prepared. To give them all a lesson. He pulled a weapon from his book bag and began firing. Up and down each aisle. All the while taking a head count.

When he finished, he walked to the front of the class, weapon by his side.

Mr. Bowers was hiding underneath his desk. And whimpering.

Crawford sat down in the teacher's chair and got comfortable. After a moment he grabbed the class roster and went to the white board. He picked up a black marker and became mathematical.

"Let's see… your class is listed as having twenty-four students. That seems accurate. Now we will calculate. Twenty-three are now dead. Minus one – me – who is not. That equals twenty-two. Isn't that right Mr. Bowers? … Hey! I'm up here you sniveling coward! Look at me when I'm talking to you. Okay. That's much …what the…really Mr. Bowers? Really? On the floor? Couldn't you have waited until the end of the class?

The Usurper

The police were baffled. There were no signs of forced entry. Both the front door and back door were locked. There were no signs of a struggle. And yet there he was. Pauly B. O'Connor. The next big singing sensation. Dead on his bedroom floor. Besides Pauly, there were only two people who had keys to his home – Timmy, his brother, and Rachel, his fiancée. Timmy was the younger of the brothers. They were polar opposites. Timmy was a computer geek with funny glasses and a crooked nose from a beating at the hands of a local gang in Queens during the "bridge wars". Timmy slept in a separate room adjacent to Pauly's. Yet when the police questioned him, he told them he heard nothing. Ever since, Timmy walked around as if in a fog with a permanent expression of fear, surprise and shock. One doctor said he was suffering from PTSD. The other diagnosed Schizophrenia.

Rachel was a curvaceous model who spent most of her time in California. She had an alibi because she was working a shoot in L.A. In three months, she would be the second Mrs. O'Connor. Pauly's unhappy ex was Frida, a local black beauty from a very religious family. Her father was a stern, holier-than-thou type of minister. Pauly's friends told him to watch out for Frieda because she was still furious that Pauly left her for a "blonde bombshell with fake tits."

The detective on the case was more interested in professional rivalry and jealousy.

Pauly was about to be crowned the "King of Rap". He had new style, was handsome and had boat loads of charisma.

Tooly Doo, an established and wealthy rapper, was one of the main suspects. Connected to one of the local gangs, he was heard mouthing off about this "silly ass cracker stealin' our spotlight, invading our turf. I mean hell we don't need no white cat getting' famous singin' our music, man."

Some of the Hip Hop insiders said they personally wondered about Funky Frank being involved somehow. Frank was the engineer and mixer for Pauly B. Everybody said he was the best in the business because he had an uncanny ability to string drum sounds from different records. Guys like Frank were the unsung heroes, the real talent behind Rap music. But Frank had an alibi too.

He was getting down with Frida at his crib.
On the evening of the murder Pauly was preparing to go to bed, alone. He pulled back the covers, propped up his pillow and turned to switch off the light.
There was the murderer with a .45 and a killer smile.
"You're a pretty boy, Pauly. Congratulations on your contract."
Despite his splendid voice, Pauly could not speak.
"Tell me son, do you believe in God?"
Pauly nodded his head, not believing what was happening.
Right before he pulled the trigger, the perpetrator said,
"Well, I don't know where the good Lord plans on sending you Pauly, but I do know of one place you're not going…and that's Graceland."
The assailant walked straight out through the front door past an astonished Timmy, who was paralyzed with fear.
To this day the murder of Pauly B. O'Connor is classified as "unsolved". There wasn't one witness who would come forward. All the forensic team could find were scuff marks from a blue suede shoe.

The Ideal Woman

I was in Paris on assignment, but I was given a day to adjust and re-orient after having spent a year in Syria. My options were limited: stand in line with five-hundred Chinese tourists at the Eiffel Tower or visit the Louvre.

Before I went to the museum, I chose to enhance my aesthetic experience by taking a hit of pure acid. I then stopped at an up-scale café for some quiche and a nice bottle of Bordeaux. The name of my server was Pierre. How's that for a nom de guerre? I spoke in impeccable French making sure to over-emphasize my American accent. Oh Pretty Pierre. I'm sure after work he exchanged his black vest for a yellow one. The French have to be the biggest complainers in the world, am I right?

By the time I got to the Louvre the acid was starting to kick in. This could get interesting.

Everyone has their favorites, right? I happen to like the Impressionists. Yes, I know that "mind blown" is a tired old cliché, but on acid the term was "le mot juste."

My next stop was Giaconda herself - LV's little masterpiece. I swear… the painting seemed to beckon to me with some mystical magnetic force. As I drew nearer, I suddenly realized why so many artists and critics believe the painting to be so extraordinary.

"My God she's beautiful!" I uttered a bit too loudly.

Her enigmatic smile instantly changed into a frown. Those gentle eyes became fierce and defiant.

She was clearly angry.

"How dare you objectify me!" she said.

"But Lisa…I'm just being honest."

"You are focusing on my physical features as if they alone define who I am. Moreover, I know what men are doing when they call you beautiful. It is an attempt at leverage over a woman. To make her self-conscious of how she looks."

I happen to love feisty women. And her sassy attitude really turned me on.

"I want to kiss you, Mona Lisa!"

At that point two security guards grabbed me by my melting arms and took me to a room with no paintings. I was still seeing colors though. They started playing fifty questions with me which was ridiculously ironic, but it was messing with my high as

well. To save my ass I had to blow my cover and confess that I worked for CNN and the CIA.
Their supervisor called the embassy and within minutes I was released with polite apologies and two free tickets to the Moulin Rouge.

Cosmic Evolution

On this third planet

our slow wobbly progress

is measured

in stumbling moments of Wow!

Each step

engendered by an unborn child

kicking with unconscious expectation

To those - now dead -

who built our cities high up on seven hills

Behold the future!

in one sudden gasp of breath

swaddled once again

into a small rocking cradle

thousands of feet above the earth

and climbing fast

to finally…finally!

walk on the moon.

Cherchez la femme

For our high school year book the editor requested that each student provide a saying to accompany their photograph. Mine read: "The right man. The wrong century."

It is certainly true. I am an 18th century type of man struggling to cope with new ways that are alien to my worldview. Truth be told, however, there is an echo of the past in every new sound.

Still… I am not at all fond of unbridled feminism. To be more precise, I greatly disapprove of women who have managed to unbridle feminism.

Once while on my way to my office, I stopped to open a door for a lovely mademoiselle.

Instead of saying "thank you", she spun around and screamed.

"What the hell are you doing?

I'm not a child – I can open the door by myself, for Christ's sake!"

It is deeply upsetting that such everyday forms of chivalry are frowned upon. But this is not my only complaint.

I happen to despise shopping for food. For each time I go through check out there is a cashier who boldly converses with me in quite a familiar fashion. As though we were of the same station in life! Although it shocks my sensibilities I simply nod and smile as if I were an aristocrat humoring a simple rustic peasant. Noblesse oblige.

My worst experience was something you may have read about.

I took my inamorata to the theatre one evening. Afterwards, we strolled along the boulevard discussing the merits of the performance. Suddenly we were accosted by a ne'er do well- a bumptious character who pronounced these very crude words…

"Damn… that is one fine looking bitch!"

It is one thing to disrespect a lady, but to do so in front of her man is quite reprehensible.

Naturally I challenged the cad to a duel. He was incredulous at first then seemed to take to the idea. For a moment I felt I may have found a kindred spirit. Someone from my century perhaps. But no, he was totally ignorant of the custom. I had to explain the rules of engagement to this lowly cur.

While doing so an unfortunate incident occurred.

I have to admit my emotions got the better of me when the blackguard interrupted me saying…

"You slap me again with that silly ass glove and I'll break your damn arm."
An affront of this magnitude could not go unanswered.
I then raised my pistolet and shot him on the spot. A terrible faux pas.
The scoundrel survived, but I was arrested and charged with a crime for which I was found guilty.
During my one-year stay, I lived rather comfortably in a private compound over-looking the sea. My residence - I must say - contained most of the amenities a gentleman might require.
All of this was made possible through fraternal assistance – my brother being Attorney General.
Plus ça change, plus c'est la même chose.
However . . . you know how life is, my friends.
Just when you think you've got it made, you have to make it all over again.
Thus, do we become cynical.
I just received word from my advocat that a woman from my past is charging me with unwanted sexual advances. It should be on the news shortly. If I heard correctly, her name is Evelyn.
I once opened a door for her.

The King of Ithaca

Joyce and Jim – both born and raised in Ithaca, N.Y. - moved into a subsidized housing complex for senior citizens around the same time.. The rooms were small, but cozy, and there was a community room with a flat screen TV, radio, games, and a computer that no one used. Until Jim arrived.

When Joyce first met Jim she got "the tingles". At sixty-five that surprised her. It made her curious and hopeful. Jim had no such reaction. Especially after the operation

Joyce gave Jim hints from time to time, but he didn't pick up on them. So she kissed him one day. Right on the lips. Jim just laughed and scooted away down the hallway to his room.

Joyce tried to interest Jim again and then a few more agains. To no avail.

She wrote touching love letters that she slipped underneath his door at night. He wrote her back that he was not pleased. In fact, he felt anxious and somewhat horrified. He pleaded with her to stop before he needed to report her.A few days later Joyce went to the community room to do something she had never done -use the computer. Jim was nearby "watching the game". Suddenly she whispered to him that she needed help because she "messed up".

The cameras in the community room were faced north to south so that anyone at the computer would be videoed from their back. Jim came over to see what was wrong and leaned over close to Joyce while trying to determine what she had "messed up". A few minutes later Joyce jumped up and ran away from Jim visibly screaming in fear with her blouse half-open as planned.

Sexual assault, of course, is a serious offence.

After the incident was investigated, Jim - evicted from the residence - forever joined the homeless such as they are.

Due to government rules Jim could not be housed in any other low-income home. His situation was quite dire.

In the years that followed, Jim lived on the street and begged outside shopping malls where he washed and used the toilet. Sometimes he stole food at the "Price Chopper" as senior citizen workers there looked the other way. Comrades in the struggle.

One December day, while outside on the freezing sidewalk, Jim saw a Community Service bus approach. The one he used to use to go shopping. From the back of the bus came Joyce being wheeled away by an attendant. Their eyes met as the attendant - pushing too hard - smacked right into his shopping cart. No one was hurt. The attendant reached into Joyce's pouch and pulling out a fifty - dollar bill said… "Miss Attina wishes for you to have this"

Joyce then shuddered and spoke with great difficulty saying "Umm zoe…ree!"

As she was wheeled away, a couple of tears fell down upon the face of Ulysses S. Grant. Jim actually thought of throwing the dollar bill into the air to let fate carry it where it may.

Then he heard the ringing bell.

He walked up to jolly old Saint Nick and handed him the fifty dollars for the Salvation Army. Penelope tugged at her white beard and thanked the kind unfortunate soul.

"Oh my…Merry Christmas!"

Standing there stunned and in disbelief she began crying from the painful joy of sorrow. Poor Ulysses nearly drowned.

"It's all relative of course"

Einstein produced "thought experiments"
Using his imagination
to discover the truth
He had to prove his imaginative ideas through science
and math. Naturally
But what if science and math are just
tricks of the imagination
like Art or Philosophy?
Or love?

ABOUT THE AUTHOR

Paul Kindlon was born in Albany, N.Y in 1952. Shortly after graduating from SUNY Albany with a B.A. in Philosophy/English Literature, he moved to Chicago and worked as a struggling stage actor for seven years. Abandoning his life in the theatre, he joined the Communist Party (CPUSA) and attended the University of Illinois at Chicago where he obtained an M.A. in Russian Literature and then a Ph.D. in Philosophy/Russian Literature in 1991. During a three month visit to Russia he fell in love, got married, and began working as a broadcast journalist. The future author traveled around Siberia through the Taiga and above the Arctic circle getting to know the country and its diverse ethnic make-up. In 1993 he was among a handful of foreign journalists allowed into the Russian Parliament to cover the historical confrontation that lead to Boris Yeltsin's consolidation of power. Having become disillusioned with journalism, he took a job as a professor at an American college in Moscow where he taught for 23 years. "It was absolute ecstasy," he says, "a dream life."

Upon retirement in late 2017, he began writing in earnest, which he refers to as . . . "that other dream life."